PRAISE FOR THE JACK SIGLER SERIES
THRESHOLD

"In Robinson's latest action fest, Jack Sigler, King of the Chess Team--a Delta Forces unit whose gonzo members take the names of chess pieces--tackles his most harrowing mission yet.Threshold elevates Robinson to the highest tier of over-the-top action authors and it delivers beyond the expectations even of his fans. The next Chess Team adventure cannot come fast enough."-- **Booklist - Starred Review**

"In Robinson's wildly inventive third Chess Team adventure (after Instinct), the U.S. president, Tom Duncan, joins the team in mortal combat against an unlikely but irresistible gang of enemies, including "regenerating capybara, Hydras, Neanderthals, [and] giant rock monsters." ...Video game on a page? Absolutely. Fast, furious unabashed fun? You bet." -- **Publishers Weekly**

"Jeremy Robinson's *Threshold* is one hell of a thriller, wildly imaginative and diabolical, which combines ancient legends and modern science into a non-stop action ride that will keep you turning the pages until the wee hours. Relentlessly gripping from start to finish, don't turn your back on this book!" -- **Douglas Preston, New York Times bestselling author of Impact and Blasphemy**

"With *Threshold* Jeremy Robinson goes pedal to the metal into very dark territory. Fast-paced, action-packed and wonderfully creepy! Highly recommended!" -- **Jonathan Maberry, *New York Times* bestselling author of *The King of Plagues* and *Rot & Ruin***

"*Threshold* is a blisteringly original tale that blends the thriller and horror genres in a smooth and satisfying hybrid mix. With his new entry in the Jack Sigler series, Jeremy Robinson plants his feet firmly on territory blazed by David Morrell and James Rollins. The perfect blend of mysticism and monsters, both human and otherwise, make *Threshold* as groundbreaking as it is riveting." -- **Jon Land,** *New York Times* **bestselling author of** *Strong Enough to Die*

"Jeremy Robinson is the next James Rollins."-- **Chris Kuzneski, New York Times bestselling author of The Lost Throne and The Prophecy**

"Jeremy Robinson's *Threshold* sets a blistering pace from the very first page and never lets up. This globe-trotting thrill ride challenges its well-crafted heroes with ancient mysteries, fantastic creatures, and epic action sequences. For readers seeking a fun rip-roaring adventure, look no further."
 -- **Boyd Morrison, bestselling author of** *The Ark*

"Robinson artfully weaves the modern day military with ancient history like no one else."-- **Dead Robot Society**

"THRESHOLD is absolutely gripping. A truly unique story mixed in with creatures and legendary figures of mythology, technology and more fast-paced action than a Jerry Bruckheimer movie. If you want fast-paced: you got it. If you want action: you got it. If you want mystery: you got it, and if you want intrigue, well, you get the idea. In short, I $@#!$% loved this one."-- **thenovelblog.com**

"As always the Chess Team is over the top of the stratosphere, but anyone who relishes an action urban fantasy thriller that combines science and mythology will want to join them for the exhilarating Pulse pumping ride."-- **Genre Go Round Reviews**

INSTINCT

"If you like thrillers original, unpredictable and chock-full of action, you are going to love Jeremy Robinson's Chess Team. INSTINCT riveted me to my chair." -- **Stephen Coonts, NY Times bestselling author of THE DISCIPLE and DEEP BLACK: ARCTIC GOLD**

"Robinson's slam-bang second Chess Team thriller [is a] a wildly inventive yarn that reads as well on the page as it would play on a computer screen."-- **Publisher's Weekly**

"Intense and full of riveting plot twists, it is Robinson's best book yet, and it should secure a place for the Chess Team on the A-list of thriller fans who like the over-the-top style of James Rollins and Matthew Reilly." -- **Booklist**

"Jeremy Robinson is a fresh new face in adventure writing and will make a mark in suspense for years to come." -- **David Lynn Golemon, NY Times bestselling author of LEGEND and EVENT**

"Instinct is a jungle fever of raw adrenaline that goes straight for the jugular."-- **Thomas Greanias, NY Times bestselling author of THE ATLANTIS PROPHECY and THE PROMISED WAR**

PULSE

"Robinson's latest reads like a video game with tons of action and lots of carnage. The combination of mythology, technology, and high-octane action proves irresistible. Gruesome and nasty in a good way, this will appeal to readers of Matthew Reilly." -- **Booklist**

"Raiders of the Lost Arc meets Tom Clancy meets Saturday matinee monster flick with myths, monsters, special ops supermen and more high tech weapons than a Bond flick. Pulse is an over-the-top, bullet-ridden good time." -- **Scott Sigler, New York Times bestselling author of CONTAGIOUS and INFECTED**

"Jeremy Robinson's latest novel, PULSE, ratchets his writing to the next level. Rocket-boosted action, brilliant speculation, and the recreation of a horror out of the mythologic past, all seamlessly blend into a rollercoaster ride of suspense and adventure. Who knew chess could be this much fun!" -- **James Rollins, New York Times bestselling author of THE LAST ORACLE**

PULSE contains all of the danger, treachery, and action a reader could wish for. Its band of heroes are gutsy and gritty. Jeremy Robinson has one wild imagination, slicing and stitching his tale together with the deft hand of a surgeon. Robinson's impressive talent is on full display in this one." -- **Steve Berry, New York Times bestselling author of THE CHARLE-MAGNE PURSUIT**

" Jeremy Robinson dares to craft old-fashioned guilty pleasures - far horizons, ancient maps, and classic monsters - hardwired for the 21st century. There's nothing timid about Robinson as he drops his readers off the cliff without a parachute and somehow manages to catch us an inch or two from doom." -- **Jeff Long, New York Times bestselling author of THE DESCENT and YEAR ZERO**

CALLSIGN:

ROOK

JEREMY ROBINSON
WITH EDWARD G. TALBOT

BREAKNECK MEDIA

Visit Jeremy Robinson on the World Wide Web at:
 www.jeremyrobinsononline.com

Visit Edward G. Talbot on the World Wide Web at:
www.edwardgtalbot.com

FICTION BY JEREMY ROBINSON

The Jack Sigler Thrillers
Threshold
Instinct
Pulse
Callsign: King
Callsign: Queen
Callsign: Rook

The Antarktos Saga
The Last Hunter - Pursuit
The Last Hunter – Descent

Writing as Jeremy Bishop
The Sentinel
Torment

Origins Editions (first five novels)
Kronos
Antarktos Rising
Beneath
Raising the Past
The Didymus Contingency

Short Stories
Insomnia

Humor
The Zombie's Way (Ike Onsoomyu)
The Ninja's Path (Kutyuso Deep)

FICTION BY EDWARD G. TALBOT

New World Orders
Alive From New York
2012: The Fifth World
Callsign: Rook

CALLSIGN:
ROOK

1

"What the hell am I doing here?"

Stan Tremblay shook his head, and his abbreviated grin carried no trace of humor. Even with half the journey behind him, the lights of the small village seemed no closer. He knew he'd get there eventually, but trekking through the far reaches of Norway's arctic in the dead of night wasn't the act of a sane man.

Tremblay's sanity wasn't the issue. A member of an elite U.S. Special Forces unit known as Chess Team, Tremblay had survived much worse than a little cold and isolation. He liked to think that his call sign, Rook, described his role on the team as the man who specialized in direct, in-your-face action. But the last mission had dispersed the five Chess Team members around the globe and Rook had lost contact with them. After the killing of his support troops by Russian helicopters, Rook had only made it out of Russia thanks to the help of an old woman with more guts than any ten civilians he'd ever met. The woman, Galya, had given her life to save his.

Right now, he didn't want to think about her. He didn't want to think about her brother, the smuggler who'd helped him escape via boat, or the other woman on the boat who had disembarked with him but now walked in the opposite direction for reasons she hadn't cared to explain. He didn't even want to think about the rest of his team, three men and one woman who were like family. He just wanted to find a warm spot to lie down and close his eyes for a few hours.

Rook sensed movement in the darkness and stopped. The moon provided enough light for him to make his way along the dirt road without a flashlight, and his eyes picked up a change in the shadows. If the source of the movement was human, the person had to know Rook was here. His hand slipped to his .50 caliber Desert Eagle pistol, one of the few things he'd managed to bring with him out of Russia. He had just five of the seven round Action Express magazines though, and he didn't have the forty-four barrel that allowed him to use the more common Magnum magazines, so he'd have to make every round count.

Multiple howls emanated from the night, and he switched on his flashlight. The light revealed a huge wolf with black fur standing a few feet away. He'd encountered wolves before during his extensive wilderness experience, and he recalled two things in particular about them. First, they tend to run away from people.

Second, they always hunt in packs.

Rook whirled, and the light picked up half a dozen more of the beasts forming a circle around him. Their coats contained the same jet-black fur as the first, but they looked smaller, more like good-sized male black labs. Unlike the first wolf, which stood still and just stared at Rook, these others growled and kept their bodies in motion. They were angling for an attack.

Rook's harsh laugh drowned out their growls. "I don't believe this shit. Okay puppies, let's see if I can't turn one of you into a nice fur-lined jacket."

He considered using the Desert Eagle, but rejected the idea

almost immediately. The sound would echo right up the fjord, possibly bringing more unwanted attention. Plus, after battling an enemy who had the ability to bring inanimate objects to life in the form of giant stone golems, dispatching the wolves with just his KA-BAR knife would not be much of a challenge.

He turned back to the large wolf and with no hesitation, sprinted straight at it. The knife was in his hand before the second step. The wolf jumped away, but not in time to avoid Rook's lunging left hand, which made contact near the animal's rib cage. A dog-like whimper lasted only an instant before an aggressive growl replaced it.

Rook pivoted and saw the large wolf now in front of the others. For a second, they locked eyes. "Didn't think a big guy like me could move like that, did you? How about I declare victory and you and the pack move on?"

As if hearing him, the wolf turned and ambled away, the other wolves following a few steps behind. The leader showed no sign of the recent injury. Rook watched them go, until even with the flashlight, he couldn't make out even the slightest trace of a bushy tail.

Rook turned off the light and continued down the road. His fatigue had disappeared, the brief action heightening his senses. The mission tonight was to find a place to sleep. He'd abandoned most of his cold weather gear during his escape, so he couldn't rest under the stars all night. If he couldn't find shelter, he'd have to keep moving.

An hour later, the road had started to tilt sharply downhill and the lights finally seemed closer. He passed two isolated shacks before reaching a larger house with a barn on one side. He saw no lights in the house—not surprising given that his watch read 2:33 a.m. He wouldn't get a better opportunity than this, especially since the barn door had only a simple latch with a padlock that was not fully engaged.

The barn smelled like any one of a hundred he'd encountered before. Rook's teenage years had included summers working on a farm in his native New Hampshire, and the odor of hay and horse dung was not unpleasant when you were accustomed to it. He allowed his lips to curl into a smirk as he considered that even above the Arctic Circle, some things don't change.

Rook could sense horses and perhaps other animals in some of the stalls, but he had no intention of spooking them by turning on his light. After allowing his eyes to adapt, he made his way to an empty stall. He'd endured far worse sleeping conditions than the pile of straw in the corner, and he drifted to sleep almost as soon as his eyelids slid shut. The Desert Eagle rested in his right hand.

His dreams included flames and explosions, from which a huge creature emerged at a full run. Rook could make out no distinct features except anger-filled yellow eyes, and he reached for his gun and tried to raise it. He couldn't move his hand, no matter how hard he tried. When he looked down, something cold and hard hit him in the nose, and his head jerked upwards.

Then his eyes opened, dispersing the remnants of the dream. One object dominated his vision. A double-barreled shotgun jammed into one of his nostrils.

2

"Good morning, soldier." The voice spoke Norwegian, a language in which Rook was fluent. Each member of Chess Team had learned at least half a dozen languages, and Rook's blue eyes and blond goatee and hair made him the natural candidate for those of northern Europe. He decided to answer rather than disarm the man pressing the shotgun into his nose.

"Yeah, good morning. You mind pointing that thing somewhere else?"

"That depends. Do you mind telling me what you're doing in my barn?"

Rook glanced up at the speaker and calculated some more. The man looked old, at least seventy to judge by the snowy hair and weathered face, but the gray eyes showed no fear or anger, just focus. A man who formerly must have commanded respect.

Rook didn't wait any longer. His right arm was inches from the end of the shotgun, and in one motion he slammed his hand into it, pushing it in one direction and rolling his body in the other direction as a counter-balance. As the gun swung away, Rook grabbed it by the barrel and jerked it out of the man's hands. The motion caused his roll to continue until he wound up kneeling, his Desert Eagle coming up into firing position.

As he aimed it, he noticed that the man had produced a small pistol. *Not a bad move*, thought Rook, *especially for a senior citizen.* He said, "I think this is what we call a standoff."

"I thought you might try something like that."

"Then why the hell did you get so close to me?"

The man chuckled. "I wanted to find out for sure." He lowered the gun to his side. "So, soldier, no more standoff. But my question stands. What are you doing in my barn?"

"I was sleeping until you shoved a shotgun in my face."

"I figured to get your attention. How did you come to be looking for a barn to sleep in, soldier?"

"Why do you keep calling me 'soldier'?"

"I've seen a few of them in my time, and you could not be anything else. Are you going to answer my question?"

Rook considered before answering. *What am I doing here, anyway?* He knew he needed some time to get right with the loss of his entire support team, but that just wasn't his style. He'd rather shoot out navels than spend time gazing at his own. But here he was.

He lowered the Desert Eagle and held out his left hand. "I wanted some time away. I started walking, and next thing I knew, I needed a place to sleep. I didn't figure I'd find a motel around here, so your barn seemed as good as anything. The name's Stanislav."

The man kept his gaze steady and didn't move to take Rook's hand. "Seems like you might have left a couple things out between walking and sleeping."

Rook laughed. "Yeah, I did. Especially the part about the wolf."

The man raised his pistol again, and Rook didn't see any wavering in the aim. "Tell me, Stanislav, what wolf are you talking about?"

Rook locked eyes with the man. "The pack of pitch-black wolves I met a few miles back, with a giant bastard the size of a small horse as their pack leader."

The man lowered the gun again, and Rook said, "Make up your mind whether you're gonna shoot me, okay? What's this all about?"

Instead of answering directly, the man asked, "These wolves, did they attack you?"

"They sure as shit would have the way they were circling me. I cut their leader with my knife and they decided to find an easier target."

Rook saw some doubt in the man's eyes for the first time. Then the man put the gun in his waistband. Rook raised his eyebrows.

"You sure you wanna put that there? You might shoot off something important."

"Son, at my age, they just are not that damn important anymore."

Rook grinned. "Fair enough. So no more standoff?"

The man reached out his hand. "If you could cut the large wolf, there never was a standoff. I would never have hit you with the gun."

Rook took the man's hand, still grinning, though he kept the Desert Eagle in the other at his side. "That's probably true. What's your name?"

"Peder Bjork. So, Stanislav, where do you come from?"

"Russia."

"Russia? I see. And when will you be moving on?"

All at once, Rook felt the urgency of the loss of contact with the rest of Chess Team. *How long had it been? Too long,* was the answer, and he needed to let them know he was only temporarily out of the game. "I don't know. A while I guess. Do you have a phone? Maybe I can figure it out myself?"

"No phones here. And before you ask, no Internet, either. Not even mail or telegram."

"I get it; we have a lot of people in, ah, Russia, who are the same way. Sometimes the damn things are more trouble than they're worth. How about someone else in town who might let me use theirs?"

"I don't think you heard me, Stanislav. In the town of Fenris Kystby, we do not have any of that."

Rook blinked.

"Are you serious? What if there was an emergency?"

"Then someone would drive an hour or two and bring help. There is really nothing we need that we cannot provide ourselves or get during occasional trips."

Rook opened his mouth to argue, then closed it. Maybe the guy was right. Maybe a few weeks with no distractions was just what he needed. He'd have to contact the team, but that could wait a little bit longer.

"I guess you're right, Peder. I'll be staying for a few days. Is there an inn or any kind of boarding house in town? Maybe a place where I won't wake up with a gun in my face?"

Peder barked a laugh. "You have a lot to learn, Stanislav. There is not anything like that. You are better off just moving on."

Rook felt the anger rising in his chest and he let his fingers flex around the Desert Eagle still at his side. "Yeah, well I like it here. I think I'll stay. You got any suggestions or are we back to a standoff?"

Peder raised his eyebrows and twisted his lips in thought. "Well now, I do have one idea. I have a little pest control problem on the farm that maybe a man like you could help with. Since you like my barn so much, I could let you sleep here for a few days in exchange for your help."

Inside, Rook groaned, his mind filled with images of chasing rats around the barn with the gun and cursing. But he had plenty of free time on his hands, and he didn't have any better options. So he nodded. "That's a generous offer, and I'll take you up on it. Thanks"

Peder said, "Are you going to put that pistol away, or are you still waiting for me to draw on you?"

Rook looked down at the gun, and tucked it into the back of his pants where it would not be seen or put his boys in danger. "Better to have it handy and not need it than the opposite."

"True, Stanislav, very true. You know, you are almost certainly the luckiest man in Fenris tonight."

"Why's that, because you didn't shoot me?"

"In a way. You're lucky you picked my barn, that's all."

"I didn't feel lucky when I first opened my eyes."

Peder chuckled. "If you had picked any other barn besides mine, you could have counted on one thing."

"What?"

"No one else in town would have woken you up before pulling the trigger."

3

After his rude awakening, Rook didn't go back to sleep. Peder gave him a brief tour of the farm, which didn't consist of much beyond the house, the barn, and some fenced enclosures for grazing. The barn housed half a dozen chickens, three cows, two pigs, two horses, and two goats, and Rook watched as Peder released them into their respective pens.

It reminded him of home in New Hampshire, which made him think of his fellow Chess Team members and how he needed to find a way to contact them. First, though, he wanted to find out more about the pest control problem Peder had mentioned. That, and get some breakfast. As Peder showed him the house proper, Rook broached the subject.

"So what exactly do you need my help with?"

Peder motioned to a faded blue couch that had seen better days. "Take a seat, Stanislav. We have a problem in this town no one wants to talk much about. Since it started taking my animals though, I've been trying to do something."

Great, Rook thought. *I'll be chasing coyotes instead of rats.* "Since what started taking your animals?"

Peder pursed his lips and looked at the peeling finish and

the wood floors. "I don't rightly know. But I used to have a dozen cows and thirty chickens. Every few days another one disappears. A couple of times I stayed up all night watching, but none ever disappeared when I was awake. One time I dozed off and when I woke up, another chicken was gone and I caught a glimpse of a huge form in the distance."

Rook looked for signs that the old man was pulling his leg, but didn't see any. He took a deep breath. "Well hell, probably just a bear or something. You ever try shooting at it?"

Peder shook his head. "I only saw it that one time. That was two days ago. When I found you this morning, I was hoping you were the culprit."

Rook grinned. "First time I've ever been accused of stealing chickens. So what exactly do you want me to do?"

Peder said, "Simple. Find whatever is doing the killing."

"And when I find it?"

Peder gestured toward the Desert Eagle in Rook's waistband. "Kill it, Stanislav. Whatever it is, kill it."

"That I can do. On a different subject, any restaurants in town where I could round up some food? I don't want to eat you out of house and barn."

"Restaurants? Not really, none that will serve outsiders."

"What kind of restaurant doesn't serve outsiders?"

"Stanislav, I told you, we like to keep to ourselves. That's why we have no outside communication. The road you came in on ends in town. The only other way to get here is a forty mile hike through rough hills covered in ice ten months a year."

"So how many outsiders do you get?"

"Not many."

"How many so far this year?"

"Including you?"

"Yeah."

"One."

Rook stood up at this and glanced out the window at the few trees in the yard blowing in the gusting wind. Then he turned back to Peder. "That's just strange—you know that, right?"

"No stranger than drinking too much vodka as a national sport like they do in your country."

Rook was confused for a second before remembering he was supposed to be Russian. "All right, all right, I see your point. My point is still that I need food, and I want to get a look at this town of yours. Do you at least have any kind of store with food? One that an outsider like me won't have to shoot my way into?"

Peder sighed. "The moment I saw you in my barn, I knew you would wind up disrupting everything. Maybe we need a little of that about now. Word will spread anyway, so I might as well introduce you to a few folks. Don't expect a big welcome hug."

"As long as I get some food, I don't give a damn what they do. You got a car or is that something else you guys can do without?"

"Of course we have cars. Mine's parked behind the barn."

"Then let's go."

Peder Bjork drove like a maniac.

The first thirty seconds, Rook enjoyed the rush, but soon it became clear that for Peder, the goal of staying on the road was entirely secondary to going as fast as possible. Rook would never have admitted it, but he felt a small bit of fear. He was at home with dangerous parachute jumps and dangerous firefights against long odds, but in this case, he had no control over the situation.

The three-mile trip descended over a thousand feet, twisting and turning the whole time, and Peder never let their speed drop below fifty miles an hour. Rook tried to focus on the clear blue water that stretched past the town to the head of the fjord, a sight that ranked among the most gorgeous he'd ever witnessed.

Peder's car was a two series Volvo, at least thirty years old, but the designers back in Sweden had never envisioned equipping it with an engine like this one. The roar coming out of the turns indicated something far different from the original four-cylinder, or even the turbo-charged fives of recent years. Rook had asked if the engine had eight cylinders, and Peder pointed his right finger in the air twice to indicate a higher number. Rook didn't want the old man to take the hand off the wheel again, so he just nodded. He could almost hear the level in the gas tank dropping.

On the surface, the town seemed a bit like a small seaside New England village, maybe one far up the coast of Maine where fewer tourists have the motivation to venture. Unlike in a New England village, not a single sign or mailbox graced the buildings. To Rook, it seemed off somehow, like waiting for Stephen King to expose a horror that lay beneath the surface. He shook off the feeling. "So where are we headed?"

As an answer, Peder mashed on the brakes, forcing Rook's seatbelt to engage as his body jerked forward. "We are here."

"I can see that now. Thanks."

They headed to a building with weathered shingles on the outside, and Peder knocked on the door. When it opened, a woman in her forties with blonde hair scowled at Peder. "What is this?"

"Anni, this is Stanislav. He has agreed to help me with the problem with my animals."

Anni opened her mouth, then closed it and moved her head once to each side. Rook couldn't tell if she was expressing disapproval, checking if someone was watching them, or both. Finally, she said, "Come on, then."

Inside, a single large room was clearly a small store, but with few labels and no prices. Rook didn't recognize most of the packaged items, but he figured he'd find plenty that he could stomach. Peder said, "Stanislav, please pick what you want."

"What about money?" Rook reached into his pocket, but Peder stopped him with a touch to his arm.

"We do not do money here, at least not the way you are used to."

"No money? You're kidding. We didn't even go that far in Russia when the Communists were in charge."

"As I said, it is different. Now please pick what you want."

The sound of the door opening made Rook turn, and he saw a man in the doorway. Solid, at well over six feet, with dark hair, cut short, the man presented an imposing figure. When his brown eyes met Rook's gaze, Rook could tell the man was accustomed to dominating those around him.

The man spoke. "So, Peder, who is this?"

Peder's voice sounded just as calm as it had all along, but Rook could sense a sort of tension. "This is Stanislav. I found him sleeping in my barn this morning, and he has agreed to help me with the problem with my animals."

"Losing a few chickens is hardly cause for concern, Peder."

"Eirek, you know it has gone beyond that. Your wolves might protect the town, but they have not stopped the beast from destroying most of what I have left."

Rook said, "Whoa there guys, let's slow down." He held out his hand to the newcomer. "I'm Stanislav. And you are?"

The man accepted his hand, but didn't bother to force a smile. "My name is Eirek Fossen. I oversee things in Fenris."

"Oversee things? Are you the mayor?"

"In a manner of speaking. As I am sure Peder has told you,

we like to take care of our own problems here. Perhaps I can help you move on to wherever it is you are headed."

Images of his fellow teammates popped into Rook's head, and he smiled. "Well, there is one thing. Peder here says you have no outside communications, but I could use a phone call or two. You wouldn't happen to have any way for me to do that, would you?"

Fossen shook his head. "Alas, no. But I would be happy to arrange for someone to drive you anywhere in Norway you want to go."

"To be honest, I kind of like it here. Clean air, a chance to unwind a bit. Really a great place. But what's this about a beast? Peder tells me of a large shadowy figure that's been gobbling up his livestock."

Behind him, he heard Anni inhale sharply. Fossen's eyebrows narrowed, and Rook could tell the disapproval was directed at her. Rook turned and saw that her hand was over her mouth and her eyes were wide with what could only have been fear.

She said, "I had no idea. Is it…*Ulverja*?"

Fossen's deep laugh didn't lighten the mood. "No, no, it is something else. The wolves have kept it at bay."

Rook returned his gaze to Fossen. "You mean that pack of wolves with the huge black leader? What do they have to do with it?"

Peder answered him. "Eirek here arranged for those wolves to protect us. At first, the beast had just roared, but after we found the second villager with his throat torn out, we had to do something, and the wolves were it. Eirek has…connections for that sort of thing."

"Enough, Peder!" Fossen's voice echoed in the room. "Stanislav, it is true that we had a problem with some sort of animal. It has not approached the town since the wolves arrived.

I am still not convinced that this creature is killing Peder's stock."

Peder's eyes remained focused at a spot on the floor, so Rook responded. "Did the wolves kill the creature?"

He watched Fossen's eyes as the man answered, and sensed that without such direct scrutiny, the man would have lied. "I don't think so, no."

"So it could be the one killing Peder's animals, right?"

"That is not your concern. Please reconsider my offer to drive you out of town. Things in Fenris can be…uncomfortable for an outsider."

"Uncomfortable is my middle name."

"I have no doubt of that. Nevertheless, I do not think you understand what I mean. It would be best if you left."

"Is that some sort of threat?"

"Take it however you like, Stanislav. Do not concern yourself in our affairs. There is a reason we have remained and will continue to remain isolated."

"Look, pal, I agreed to help Peder find what's killing his cows and chickens. Since you don't seem to have any answers for him, I don't see what the problem is. Worst thing that happens is I'm here for a little while and everyone gets to point and whisper."

Fossen stepped closer, so his face was only a foot from Rook's. Rook didn't often face someone who could look down on him, but the town's leader did by just a little bit. "Stanislav, that is not anywhere near the worst thing that could happen. Consider my advice. Consider it seriously."

With this, Fossen looked at Anni. "Give him what he wants." Then he turned and left, ducking his head slightly in the doorway.

Rook looked at the other two. Peder looked fine, but Anni's face had gone even paler than the color that naturally accompanied her light hair and blue eyes. He shook his head. "That guy was a laugh a minute. Who voted for him, anyway?"

Anni's voice contained no inflection. "Everyone."

Peder cleared his throat. "Look Stanislav, we will talk more about him later. Just get your food and let's go."

Fifteen minutes later, they returned to the Volvo carrying three burlap bags. On the way out, Peder had apologized to Anni for their coming by. As Peder started the car, Rook looked at him.

"What the hell was that all about?"

"Eirek is in charge. He has been for a long time. Before that, it was his father. He gets things done here, but he also has to have them done his own way."

"That sucks."

"It is the way in this town, Stanislav."

Rook inhaled through his nose. It figured that he'd wind up in the most remote town in Europe in the middle of more dysfunction than a daytime talk show. "Fine. What about the beast you were talking about?"

"Yes, the beast. Despite what Eirek says, I am certain it is the same thing that killed the two people in town. I have heard the roar."

"And the wolves supposedly keep it away from town?"

"Supposedly. Whatever they are doing, it is not working up at my place."

"So what do you think it is?"

"If I told you, you would say I was crazy."

"Trust me, if you knew the shit I've seen the past year, you wouldn't worry."

"All right. It was dark, but I did get a pretty good look at the back of it from about thirty feet away. It was nine feet tall and it was running on two legs."

"Wait a minute, it was a man?"

Peder shook his head and put the car in gear. Rook tried to look natural putting one hand on the dashboard to brace himself for the ride home.

"No Stanislav, it was not a man. Not that tall, and not with such long arms. I could not say exactly, but there are legends about this sort of creature. In Asia, they call it the *yeti*. But the most frequent sightings are in North America.

"In America, they call it Bigfoot."

4

Bigfoot.

Rook hadn't known whether to laugh or give Peder a whack on the head to knock some sense into him. Bigfoot, or the yeti, weren't any more insane than giant stone golems coming to life, but Rook hadn't believed those either, until he'd seen them with his own eyes. Of course, he had seen something similar in the mountains of Vietnam. Red and the old mothers could have easily passed for yeti. The Neanderthal descendants were a little shorter than the legend, but they still packed a punch, and Rook had the scars to prove it. He wondered if this was something similar, but decided that it was more likely some kind of rabid animal was on the loose here, and people were seeing monsters in their imagination.

Except that people were acting damn strange. Peder, he could write off as a man old enough not to care if he lost a marble or three, but what about Anni and Eirek? The woman was terrified of something, and the town's leader had tried far too hard to get rid of Rook. Something was rotten in Norway.

When they got back to the house, Peder allowed Rook to use the kitchen to cook himself a meal. As he boiled rice over the propane stove, he chuckled to think of the ribbing he'd take from his teammates if they knew. Back home, Rook avoided the kitchen whenever he could, and Queen in particular would have taken great delight in questioning his manhood if she could have seen him now.

At the thought of Queen, his mood grew heavier. Sooner or later, he'd have to deal with the tension between them— tension that might be good if their jobs involved something other than fighting long odds to save the world. First, though, he had to contact his team, something that wasn't going to happen as long as he stayed here.

He shook off the self-analysis. It didn't do any good to beat himself up or give in to his uncertainty. He was here now, and he had a mythical creature to defeat. Or maybe just a rabid bear; he didn't care as long as he was on the delivery side of some ass-kicking. Eirek Fossen could use a well-delivered smackdown as well. Maybe teach him not to be such an asshole.

As they sat down at an ancient, crack-filled table constructed from teak, Rook asked Peder a question that had occurred to him on the slightly less precarious drive back up the hill.

"That woman, Anni, mentioned a word, *Ulverja*. What does that mean?"

Peder's fork stopped halfway to his mouth. He returned it to the bowl and raised his eyes. "Stanislav, there are some secrets in this town that it is best you stay ignorant of. But I will tell you what *Ulverja* means in our mythology. Have you heard of the Dire Wolves?"

Rook nodded. You couldn't get his kind of extensive training in the Norwegian language without coming across that. "Sure. Huge beasts that served the Norse Gods, right? I seem to recall that some think that they were intended as symbols of human suffering, but mostly I remember them being vicious killers."

"That's right. *Ulverja* was an outcast wolf, too nasty even for the others of his kind. And that is all I'm going to tell you."

Rook didn't get any sense that the old man was willing to give in. "That'll do, at least for now. But some weird shit is going on in this town. Maybe it's just the isolation, but I think there's more to it. You know I won't stop poking around."

"You will if they kill you first."

"Right. What are they gonna do, come after me with pitchforks and torches while I'm asleep in the barn?"

"No, they prefer a quiet throat slitting around three in the morning."

Rook looked for a sign that Peder was joking and found none. "So they're going to try sneak up on me and cut my throat? A perfect stranger who hasn't done anything to them?"

Peder's eyes seemed dead when they met Rook's. "They have done it before."

That night, Rook put Plan A into effect. Peder had waited in different spots on different evenings, keeping an eye on his animals and anyone who might approach them. Rook couldn't stand to be that passive, so he had talked Peder into doing something different.

First, they placed cows or goats at the furthest corners of the property. This should increase the temptation for the creature to strike. Second, they both retired to the house a couple hours after darkness set in. Rook crept out another hour later, exiting through a cellar door that provided darkness so complete he could not see his hand in front of his face.

Rook thought of the equipment Chess Team had available, the suits constructed using stealth technology that would have made him nearly invisible. Tonight, he was going old school, wearing a black jacket and pants, with some of Peder's thick axle grease smeared on his face and the backs of his hands. He knew that most animals would sense him by smell instead of sight anyway, but he'd take any small advantage he could get.

Earlier in the day, Peder and Rook had walked for miles through the land surrounding the property. They had found no sign of any of the bodies of Peder's lost chickens, goats or cows. This seemed odd, as most predators do not travel far with their captured prey unless they need to feed offspring. The risks of trouble are too great, so most predators opt to eat their meal as soon as they can do so safely. Plus, even for a bear, carrying a dead cow just didn't seem likely.

So he might be facing something with the intelligence to plan ahead. Rook had questioned Peder about whether any of the townspeople might be behind it, but Peder denied any possibility of that, saying that Fossen would never have stood for such a disruptive situation. That left…well, it didn't leave much, and Rook wasn't about to accept the yeti theory at face value.

He prepared himself for the unknown, something his time with Chess Team had exposed him to on a regular basis. In truth, he relished it. He might be in a tiny town in Norway with only a KA-BAR and a fifty caliber pistol, and the stakes might only be some livestock, but it didn't matter. Tonight, he would hunt again.

He began walking in loops, leaving and entering Peder's property numerous times. He tried never to stray too far from the corners where the goats and cows were strategically placed. Peder would be in the barn by now, hidden in the loft with a shotgun trained on the unlatched door. Rook knew that they could lose one of the outdoor animals if the attacker were smart and followed Rook's movements, but he was banking on the change of strategy to increase the likelihood of catching it—

whatever it was—in an exposed position.

Nothing happened until about two in the morning. Then, as Rook passed by one of the goats and started to leave it behind, he heard something. Just the faintest trace of sound, but still something different from the wind he'd listened to since beginning his rounds. He stopped and sniffed the air.

He picked up a smell, something like rotten eggs, but even sharper. As he inhaled, the smell grew stronger, as if the source had moved nearer. He turned his body slowly until he could see back in the direction of the goat, though the darkness prevented him from actually seeing the unfortunate animal.

His hand flexed on the Desert Eagle as the smell became even worse. He couldn't have said how he knew, but the source of the odor seemed to be in the same direction as the goat. He envisioned a large creature, unaware of Rook's presence, moving in for the kill. If Rook could just find the right place to aim…

Instead Rook let out a roar and started sprinting toward the goat. Then he switched on his light. Lying in wait to try to shoot something he couldn't even see would never work, and in any case, Rook preferred the direct approach.

A second later, he heard a roar in response that was loud enough to drown out everything else, even the sound of his own breathing. The light shone on a huge creature standing on two legs. At least eight feet tall and as thick as a hundred year old maple tree, the massive beast had brown fur that almost seemed orange in the light. *Definitely bigger than Red*, Rook thought, comparing the creature to the Neanderthal queen that had tried to take him as her own. The roar got even louder, and Rook could see huge teeth in the open mouth, mostly flat but with pointed canines. Then it started sprinting toward him.

Rook fired three shots with the Desert Eagle. The range was only about forty feet, but between the disorientation caused by the roar and the mix of light and darkness, he suspected only one shot hit home. With quickness foreign to such a huge mass, the beast turned and started running the other direction. Rook got off a couple more rounds, but neither of them hit, and he didn't want to waste the two remaining shots in the magazine on low percentage shots.

He continued the chase, but he could sense the distance between them increasing. As the flashlight swung forward with each pump of his arm, it shone on the fleeing giant, but when his arm swung back, he could no longer see it. He tried to get more onto his toes to squeeze every ounce of speed out of his legs, but he knew he could only maintain the burst for a few seconds.

Suddenly, the creature seemed to dart to the right. Rook tried to estimate the path it had taken and follow, but a tingling in his head told him he was missing something. He grabbed onto the only small tree in the area as he tried to change directions, and his legs flew forward even as his hands and arms held him in place. His legs floated for a second before dropping.

And hit nothing but air.

The slick grease on his hands served as good camouflage but now it betrayed him. His hands slid down the tree and he tried to reach further up to lock his hands around his forearms. He managed it, but only just in time for his chin to smash into the dirt. His legs…well he'd now figured out where he was. His legs and torso dangled off the side of a cliff.

He'd seen this place earlier, the far edge of Peder's land, where the earth surrendered to a two hundred foot drop down to the ocean's rocky edge. Now, a single narrow tree was all that kept his considerable bulk from a free fall. His arms started to burn, and he tried to pull himself up.

He knew the first foot or so was the hardest, and he let out two or three curses that sounded neither Norwegian nor Russian. He didn't care about that just now, he cared about getting his ass back onto solid ground. Soon enough, his strength prevailed, and he pulled himself over the top.

He got to his feet almost immediately, breathing in great lungfuls of air as he did so. The creature could still be around. He could see the flashlight a few feet away and he pounced on it. With the light, he found the Desert Eagle as well. He had dropped both mere feet from the cliff's edge, and he knew that only luck could explain why neither had gone over.

Rook sniffed the air, and the rotting smell seemed a lot less strong. He suspected the smell emanated from the creature, and its diminution meant that his quarry was still on the run. The odds of engagement again tonight were low, and he knew that even for future nights, he'd lost the element of surprise. Hell, one of his bullets was in the bastard's leg, something no animal would forget.

For tonight, he had only one option left: Return to the barn.

Five minutes later, he opened the barn door, calling out before he stepped in.

"Peder, it's me, don't shoot."

Rook shined the flashlight into the loft and saw the old man stand and head for the ladder. He went to meet him.

"What a goddamn night."

Peder looked at him, "Did you get him?"

"That depends on what you mean. I hit him with one of my shots."

"Then what happened?"

"Didn't slow him down, not even a little bit. The son of a bitch was roaring like a son of a bitch. As soon as I hit him, he turned and ran, and I couldn't keep up. I tried, but I had no chance."

"So what is it?"

He looked at Peder, and could see excitement in the man's

eyes. Rook shook his head. "I have no idea. It looked just like you described, eight feet tall, fur, huge arms and legs. But its teeth looked sort of human, and the eyes showed some definite intelligence."

Peder nodded. "Like I said. *Yeti* or whatever you want to call it. Did you smell the smell?"

"Damn right I did. That was one foul stench. And before you say it, yeah I know a lot of the legends talk about a foul smell. I'm not buying it. There's something more going on here. Maybe related to some of those secrets you don't want to tell me about. Maybe something about wolves. You almost shot me that first night when I said I saw the wolves."

Peder let himself down onto a hay-covered seat against the wall and fixed his eyes on the floor. "Stanislav, there are things I simply can't tell you."

"Tell me this, then. Why do you think the wolves keep the creature away from town but not your place?"

"I do not know. I do not know how wolves could stop a creature like that anyway."

"You're right, there's no way they could. How did anyone come up with the idea that they were?"

"It was Eirek. He is the one that told us he had managed to get the wolves and they would stop it."

"And this made sense to you?"

"You have to know Eirek. This is the kind of thing he does. Even now, I do not have any doubts about that."

"Well you should. There's something he's not telling you, even beyond whatever secrets you're holding back."

"If you are right, Stanislav, then what is it?"

Rook inhaled through his nose. "I don't know, but I intend to find out. I just thought of Plan B."

"What does this mean, 'Plan B'?"

Rook chuckled. "It's an American expression that made its

way to Russia a while back. Plan A is the first choice, Plan B is the second choice."

"And if Plan B fails?"

"Hell, in Russia we have thirty-three letters in the alphabet, so we keep on going down the list."

"All right, Stanislav. What is your Plan B?"

"I won't be able to kill the beast unless I get lucky. I doubt even the fifty caliber bullets would penetrate that thick skull. I'll either have to unload a whole magazine into its legs and hope they do enough damage to take it down, or get close enough to shoot through the eyes or under the chin. None of those seem likely. So I need to go at this from another angle. Those wolves are part of all this, making Plan B pretty simple.

"Tomorrow night, I capture the wolves."

5

Rook lay down in his bed of hay just after three in the morning. One of the old-timers had told him right when he was starting out in the military that for any soldier, sleep is a weapon. Use it when you have the chance and you never know when it might give you a small edge. Rook fell asleep in just a few seconds.

He didn't dream this time. His eyes opened some time later, and he sensed…a disruption. Maybe a noise had woken him up. He didn't move, but he listened for any additional sound. He heard none.

A minute later, he tried to close his eyes again. This time though, he couldn't fall asleep. The back of his neck tingled with the sense that he was missing something. *Screw this*, he thought. In one motion, he grabbed the Desert Eagle and switched on the flashlight.

A man stood over him, a straight razor in his hand.

Rook fired a shot, but the light had caused the intruder to stumble enough that the shot went wide. Rook cursed and jumped to his feet. The man's arm swung back, and then he flung the razor sidearm at Rook. Rook raised the flashlight to block the blade, and it bounced off the flashlight and nicked him on the chin. He felt no pain, but he roared in anger and redirected the flashlight.

The intruder was running, almost at the barn door. Rook raised the Desert Eagle, but the man ducked behind a large cart with a frame of iron and wooden sides. The bullets would penetrate, but probably wouldn't do much damage, especially if the man had crouched behind the wheels.

Rook growled, and thought, *Fine, no problem. Try to cut me, I'll settle this the old fashioned way.*

He charged at the cart, but then had to dodge a huge saddle that came flying over the top of the cart at him. During that second, the intruder made a bid to cover the four feet left to the door.

Even off-balance, Rook fired the Desert Eagle. He didn't have the angle for a reliable torso shot or the stability for a head shot, but he put a bullet in the vicinity of the man's legs. A scream of pain confirmed that it had found its target, but the tall figure disappeared out the door anyway, slamming it closed behind him.

Rook sprinted for the door, ripped it open and then paused. He replaced the now empty magazine with a fresh one, and caught his breath. If the guy had anything else to throw at him, waiting a second might draw him out. Nothing came, so Rook burst through the doorway and leaped to his right. The flashlight illuminated the man, as tall as Rook and dressed in black. He had only managed to get fifteen feet away, hampered by a limp that appeared to affect both legs.

Satisfied that the shot had struck flesh, Rook pounced. A few steps and he crossed his forearms and delivered a tackle any middle linebacker would have appreciated. The man's cry contained unmistakable pain, and his legs slipped out from under him as his face planted in the frozen dirt. Rook dropped, drove a knee into the man's back and pushed his hand into the back of the man's head, forcing it further into the ground.

Despite his anger, Rook did remember to speak in Norwegian. "Who the hell are you?"

He couldn't make out the muffled response, so he flipped the man over. He put his knee on the man's chest and stuck the Desert Eagle under his chin. "Answer the question."

"Fuck you."

Rook put down the flashlight and let his fist smash into the man's nose. When he picked up the light again, blood streamed from both nostrils. "Let's try that again."

"I am going to kill you, foreign asshole. Do not ever close your eyes."

"And why would you want to do that?"

The man spit in his face, and Rook could feel the saliva dripping down his eyelid. "We do not want your kind here. You are filth that needs to be cleaned."

"Look who's talking, pal."

Rook had known that trying to pin a strong man to the ground while holding a flashlight in one hand and a pistol in another was risky. So he wasn't shocked when the man's hand shot up, holding some sort of knife. Rook dropped the flashlight and grabbed the man's wrist to keep the knife away. Rook literally had the upper hand, and he could feel the man's resistance failing.

A second later, the resistance stopped. The knife dropped as if the man were pulling it toward himself. With only a wayward beam from the dropped flashlight for illumination, he couldn't make out exactly how it happened, but the intent seemed clear enough: The man had turned the blade on himself.

Rook tried to pull back on the man's wrist, but it was too late. The knife buried itself in the man's throat, and Rook felt warm blood spurt onto his hand. As his hand finally pulled the knife away, some drops of blood landed on his cheek. The smell hit a few seconds later, a heavy odor that reminded Rook of so many prior battles.

He grabbed the flashlight. The man's eyes had opened wide, but the gash in his throat and the huge volume of blood still leaking out confirmed the only possible outcome: The intruder was dead.

Rook stood up, still holding the gun and flashlight.

"Damn it!" He swore in English. Corpses didn't often answer questions. *Where's Richard Ridley when you need him*, Rook thought. Ridley, as head of the now shutdown Manifold Genetics, had not only developed a serum that regenerated the human body and extended life indefinitely, but he could also animate the inanimate. Rook wondered if that applied to dead bodies, too.

A moment later, a light came on near the door of the house, and Peder came out. "You okay, Stanislav? I heard the shots."

"Yeah, Peder, I'm fine. This guy here, though, he's not doing so well."

Peder reached the body, and when he saw it, he gasped. "Dear God, what have you done?"

"I didn't do anything. He cut his own throat."

"Please, Stanislav, do not take me for a fool."

Rook raised his voice. "Hey, it's the damn truth. I woke up with him standing over me with a razor. He ran when I shined the light in his face, and I hit him in the legs with a shot. I was trying to find out why he wanted to kill me, then he tried to hit me with another knife. When he couldn't do that, he slashed his own throat with it."

Peder stared at the body, shaking his head. "This is very, very bad."

"I don't know; I'm still alive. That's got to count for something."

"Stanislav, do you know who this is?"

"No, who?"

"The man you just killed? This is Jens Fossen."

"Wait a minute. You don't mean…?"

"Yes. This is Eirek Fossen's son."

"I'll fucking kill him."

"Stanislav, you already killed him."

"Not Jens. Eirek. You said it yourself that Dad runs this town. There's no way Junior came up here on his own."

"Stanislav, killing Fossen is not a good idea."

"Sure it is. I might be a stranger in this town, but when someone tries to kill me the first night I'm here, I'm gonna respond. You guys'll be better off without your own little Stalin telling you what to do."

"You do not understand me. Killing Fossen will unleash terrible things."

"Come on, what terrible things? How bad can it be?" Even as he said it, Rook knew he didn't mean those words. He'd seen some stuff that made disaster movies look like uplifting films. But some dude in a small town in Norway couldn't possibly be that bad.

"You don't know Eirek Fossen. He is a scientist. He has discovered both terrible and wonderful things. And that is all I can say about it."

Rook sighed. "After I kill him, you'll feel different."

Peder shook his head. "No. Stanislav, I begged you to leave, but you did not. Now I beg you, do not try this."

"Look, he's dead, end of story. We have to figure something else out. What do we do with the body? We need to dispose of it where no one will ever find it."

Peder frowned. "The ground is too hard to dig. I do not think we can rely on animals to do the job. How about the ocean?"

"I don't know the currents around here, but too much

chance of it floating somewhere. I guess we'll just have to burn it."

Peder met Rook's eye. "We cannot create a fire in my stove hot enough to burn the bones."

"It'll be hot enough to serve our purpose. It's a crappy job, but the alternative is that someone finds out. Better everyone thinks he disappeared, especially Eirek."

Peder didn't say a word. Instead he dipped his head in a nod, then turned and walked slowly to the house. Unlike the first time Rook had seen him, the old man looked his age, a frail and tired specimen nearing the end of things. Rook felt a small bit of regret, but not a lot. Things would probably get worse before they got better. "Story of my life," he muttered under his breath.

Then he looked down at the body. The flow of blood was slow now, just a gradual oozing. Soon it would stop entirely. Nevertheless, he needed some sort of old blanket or sheet to wrap the body in to avoid getting blood anywhere else. He followed Peder into the house to ask for one.

By nine in the morning, they'd taken care of the body. Plenty of charred bones remained, but those Peder would drive twenty miles up the road and scatter into the water at various locations. The specifics of how they managed the burning—well, Rook preferred not to think about those ever again if possible.

Rook could feel the fatigue from two nights of no sleep weighing on him. So he made his way into the barn and lay down on his blanket in the hay.

He could hear low sounds from the animals in the barn, and it helped calm his mind as he closed his eyes. Just before falling asleep, he could have sworn he heard a faint roar in the distance, the sound of the creature carrying from several miles away.

Then again, he might have just been dreaming.

6

Rook returned to town in the middle of the afternoon. Peder had allowed him to take the car, but had refused to come along.

"No, Stanislav. I am an old man, so I will not try to stop you, but I will not be part of it."

Four hours of sleep had served only to fuel Rook's anger. Between a mysterious creature that could shrug off a fifty caliber round and a man who would rather take his own life than answer questions, the town had proven far from a quiet place to hide. Now it was time to take the action right to the source of power: Eirek Fossen.

By sending his son, the man might as well have tried to pull the trigger himself. In Rook's world, such men needed to be confronted sooner rather than later. You never gave someone an extra chance to take you out.

Rook parked outside Anni's store, just as Peder had done the previous day. He didn't know where Fossen lived, but he figured all he had to do was show up in town and the man would find him. So he leaned against the car, crossed his arms, and stared out at the waves crashing into the sharp rocks a few feet past the other side of the road.

Fossen showed up a minute later. Walking down the street, he seemed even larger, one of the few men at whom Rook did not have to look down to make eye contact. Rook thought he'd glimpsed a door closing at a house a few doors down behind Fossen, and filed away the information for future use.

Rook stood with his hands at his sides, but he knew he could draw, aim, and fire the Desert Eagle in less time than it took most people to blink. Gunning the man down in the middle of the street wasn't his first choice, but he didn't have a problem if it went down that way. Despite Peder's warnings, Rook suspected that killing Fossen would actually solve more than just his own problem, and not every resident would shed a tear at Fossen's demise.

The taller man stopped a few feet away, smiled, and opened his arms in a welcoming gesture. "Stanislav, it is good to see you again. Allow me to apologize if I was rude yesterday. It was no way to welcome a visitor."

Rook blinked. Of all the ways he'd considered Fossen might react to Rook's return to town, this one had never crossed his mind.

No way, he thought. *The bastard is up to something.*

Rook said, "You told me yesterday to get out of town or something bad could happen to me. You didn't want any visitors. The threat was pretty direct."

Fossen pursed his lips and dropped his chin. "As I said, please forgive me. It is rare to have someone visit, and I was in a bad mood yesterday. I should have realized that having someone else to work on our little problem could only help."

Fossen took a step closer and held out his hand. For a second, Rook was torn. Should he just shoot the man and get it over with? He couldn't do it, not with Fossen in front of him smiling and trying to shake his hand, never mind the fact that shooting people—even assholes—in cold blood broke his own personal code of ethics.

There's no way he knows about his son, Rook thought. *He couldn't be that good of an actor.*

So if Fossen had sent his son to kill Rook, and here Rook was, what did the town's leader think had happened? It didn't make any sense. Sometimes, situations demanded shooting first and asking questions later, but this didn't seem like one of those times.

Rook shook Fossen's hand. "I'm glad to hear that, I guess." When he met Fossen's eyes, he didn't see any deception, though he saw the same power he'd noticed the previous day. He wouldn't kill the man, but trust…? Well, Rook would watch his back every second in this town, Fossen's apparent change of heart notwithstanding.

As they shook hands, Fossen seemed to scrutinize Rook's face. "Where are you from?"

Rook wondered if the man was on to him. "Russia."

"Yes," Fossen said. "I mean originally. Your lineage."

Rook saw no reason to lie about that, so he told the truth. "My father was born in Germany. My mother in Sweden. Both families immigrated to…Russia, and my parents met in school."

"I sensed you had a strong bloodline," Fossen said, looking strangely pleased. But his lips turned down slightly. "Though it is strange. Immigrating to Russia? I can't help wondering why."

"You and me both," Rook said. "It's a family mystery I'm afraid." The truth, of course, was that both families had immigrated to the United States, as many families at the time did. If Fossen suspected the lie, he didn't press it.

"I had my first encounter with the creature last night," Rook said, changing the subject. "Have you seen it?"

"Yes, one time. After the first killing. We have not had a murder here in two decades, and people were very upset. That night, my son Jens and I patrolled the area to see what we could learn. The moon was full and I smelled the stench right before I saw it. As soon as it recognized me, it ran away, faster than you would think possible."

Rook said, "Oh, I saw the bastard coming at full speed toward me—I know about fast. What do you mean it recognized you?"

"I am sorry, I meant it saw me. As soon as it saw me, it ran. What did you do when it came at you?"

"I put a bullet in its leg. It changed directions but hardly slowed at all, like the bullet didn't even hurt it."

Fossen's eyebrows showed a trace of surprise. "You hit it? Really? That is more than any of us have managed."

"Yeah, well, the thing can outrun me in its sleep, and I doubt I'll get so lucky again. Do you have any idea what it is?"

"I do not know. We are an unusual town, but a monster such as this…" Fossen held his palms up, "…is beyond our experience."

Rook thought he detected something in Fossen's voice, a sign that his answer didn't constitute the whole truth. No surprise there. He decided not to pursue it. "I've had an experience or three, but I can't say I've ever seen a guy built like a tree who can run like a cheetah and smells like Satan's asshole. So tell me about the wolves. How do they fit in?"

"The wolves." Fossen eyes darted to the ground for a second. "That will take a few minutes to explain. Why don't you come back to the house? We will have some tea and I will tell you the whole story."

Rook stifled a laugh. No way he'd hear the whole story about anything. Tea with Fossen could be more hazardous to his health than chain-smoking unfiltered Russian cigarettes. Still, he had no other options.

"Sure, that sounds fine."

"Then come this way." Fossen turned back the way he had

come. Rook followed, glancing at the houses as he passed them. He noticed one disturbing thing. Every single house had at least once face pressed to the glass of a window.

They were watching him.

"So you want to know about the wolves?" Fossen didn't waste any time getting to the point after a woman—possibly his wife, Rook wasn't sure—brought their tea into the living room. Rook considered this directness one small point in the man's favor.

"Seems like a good idea."

"Very well. It might seem odd in such an isolated town, but I am a scientist by trade. I have a small lab where I study animals, with a special focus on wolves."

"Why wolves?"

"Why not? I could bore you with the details of how I came to be interested in them, but let us just say that we can learn a lot about human beings from them. In any case, I always have a few live specimens around, and it happens that this year I took possession of a particularly large male. He was the result of some very selective breeding focused on large size, and while he is closest to a Russian wolf, he is technically something unique."

"So that must be the black wolf I saw. I didn't know black wolves existed."

"Oh, there have always been black wolves, but they are not common. And a wolf this size is something close to the largest one recorded since the dire wolves became extinct."

Rook noted a trace of sadness in Fossen's voice. Odd for someone who seemed like such a hard case. "He was huge, I'll agree with that. So tell me, what does your research have to do with our massive predator? You're not suggesting that it is a wolf?"

Fossen laughed. "Of course not. No, where the wolves

come in is that part of my research has been on seeing how the wolves react to different stimuli. I have discovered that certain smells drive the large one into a murderous frenzy. Any significant amount of blood does it, as does raw meat. The interesting thing is that after identifying the source of the smell, the wolf directs its aggression on whatever people or animals are closest to it. My assistant and I each sustained a bite before we figured this out. The rest of our wolves do not have this reaction on their own, but when they are with the large wolf, they will follow his example and also attack."

Despite his distrust, Rook found himself interested in the story. He'd seen the wolf up close, and it seemed different, more in control than most wild animals he'd encountered. Yet Fossen was describing far different behavior. He thought he knew what came next in the story.

"That's an unusual reaction. Let me guess, after the second killing, you wondered if perhaps the horrible smell emanating from the creature would trigger the same aggressive reaction in the wolves?"

"Yes I did. I had to do something, and it also served to help me figure out where to go next with the research. Obviously any scientific controls are non-existent now, but what I learn could wind up being critical."

"You released the wolves. What happened next?"

"That night, at about midnight, the whole town heard a terrifying roar coming from somewhere not too far from town. The next morning, I went out to look for the wolves. They are outfitted with implants so I can track them. I found one of them dead, its neck snapped, and with teeth marks around the shoulder and belly. Teeth marks not from a carnivore but from some sort of massive primate. The rest of the wolves stood around it in a circle, as if protecting their dead companion. I have heard of such behavior on rare occasions, but never seen it myself."

"So the creature killed one of the wolves. What makes you think they're keeping it at bay?"

"I followed the trail the wolves had taken to get to this point, and a half mile away, I found several chunks of flesh with brown and orange fur. The smell on the flesh confirmed that it could only have come from our creature. The wolves had to have hurt it. And ever since that day, I have allowed them to roam, and the creature has not come back."

"Are you sure?"

"I am sure it has not killed anyone else. It does seem to be targeting Peder's farm, and I have no idea why."

"Yeah, that does seem strange. But the whole thing is strange. You just happen to be targeted by some freak of nature, then you happen to have a pack of wolves handy with a leader who will attack the creature as soon as he gets a whiff of its stink. There's something you're not telling me, or at least some clue we're missing."

Fossen's face turned a little bit red. "I have told you all I can about my research without breaking confidences. There is nothing else you need to know. As for the creature, your guess is as good as mine."

Rook stared at Fossen and didn't say a word. The Norwegian didn't blink, didn't show any sign of discomfort beyond the red face. Finally, Rook sighed.

"Well, I don't know that I'm any better off than I was. My original plan was to capture the big wolf. It sounds like that won't tell us anything you don't already know. What about tracking it? Do you have any sense of whether it has encountered the creature, based on where it roams?"

"I have been trying to analyze the movement patterns. Every night except one or two, there has been a short period of time where the pack is sprinting at top speed. Maybe this is when they are tracking the creature. Perhaps if we follow them at a distance, but move in when we see this speed increase, we would find the creature."

Rook snorted. "And then what? It'll take more than just a guy with a gun to bring this thing down. Do you have anything more substantial that we can fire from a distance, something at least semi-automatic?"

"We do have one or two things that might be of use. How about an AR-15?"

"Yep, that would probably do it. Semi-automatic."

"Actually, I have the auto sear for it."

Rook raised his eyebrows. "You've got an AR-15 converted to fully automatic? What do you need that for?"

"I have more than one. We are isolated out here. You never know what sort of threats will come along."

"Given what I saw last night, I can't argue with that."

"Great. So what time do you want to meet to go after it?"

"Whoa. We definitely need your tracking device, but I go out into the field alone."

Fossen's voice rose. "You are not in a position to be making that kind of demand."

"Oh no? Do you want my help or not?"

The older man was silent. Rook said, "I thought so. It's nothing personal. You just show me how your tracking device works and I'll do the rest."

"No, you will not. The device I have is large and needs to stay in one place. I can keep in touch with you by walkie-talkie."

"Walkie-talkie? I thought you didn't have any outside communication?"

"These things have a range of about ten miles. They hardly qualify. I can tell you where the wolves are and you can follow at a distance where they will not know you're there."

"And you'll also give me the weapon, right?"

Fossen's eyes narrowed. "Yes, I will. But you understand that I am trusting you?"

"Sure, like I'm trusting you. For all I know, you've poisoned my tea."

Fossen's laugh boomed. "You are a funny man. There is one thing I know for certain."

Fossen looked serious, and Rook couldn't shake a sense of threat, but he played along. "Yeah, what's that?"

"The death of a man like you will not be from drinking a cup of poisoned tea."

7

Rook's thoughts turned to his team as he drove back up the hill. He wondered what Queen would do about Fossen if she were in Rook's shoes. *Probably threaten to cut his balls off if he didn't spill everything.*

Rook missed her, missed the whole team, but he didn't quite feel ready to rejoin the real world. Sure, if he had a phone, he'd let them know where he was, but the loss of his team in Russia still weighed on him. He needed to focus on the current mission.

Right now, Fossen was helping him, and he was curious what the town's leader was up to. Fossen feeding him information via walkie-talkie wouldn't exactly be like Chess Team's Deep Blue. Deep Blue had guided most of their missions, his satellite capabilities and worldwide contacts acting like eyes above the battlefield. When they had learned Deep Blue's identity—the recently resigned President of the United States—it had all made sense. No, Fossen wasn't Deep Blue, but Rook would take any advantage he could get.

Back at the house, Peder was absent. With darkness almost complete already, Rook retired to the barn for some more rest before Fossen would meet him there at ten that night to deliver the walkie-talkie and the AR-15. He closed his eyes and let sleep take over.

He was awakened by the sound of gravel crunching under car tires. His watch said eight o'clock, so he roused himself, grabbed a flashlight, and poked his head out the door. Peder was slamming the door of another Volvo, which then drove off. Rook shined the flashlight in the old man's direction.

Peder held his hands to his eyes. "Stanislav? Is that you?"

"Yep. Welcome home."

Peder approached the barn. "Thank you, son. I understand things did not go as planned with Eirek."

"You could say that. The man was so damn reasonable; he was like a different person from yesterday."

Peder nodded. "He can be like that. I do not bother to try to figure out what is going on in his head. He has done great things for this town though."

"Like what?"

"A ways back, he convinced the Norwegian government to fund a geothermal power plant for us. Before that, the old above-ground lines were always breaking down, leaving us without power for days at a time. Now, we have the most reliable power in the nation. I still do not know how he pulled it off."

"What about his research? Do you know anything about that?"

Peder's voice carried caution. "What did he tell you about his research?"

"That he specializes in wolves, how they interact with their environment, how humans can learn things from studying them."

"That sounds about right. Do not ask me the details, I'm just a farmer."

"Just a farmer. I'll bet my pension that you used to be more than just a farmer."

"Perhaps I was. In any case, Fossen's research is his business."

Rook shook his head and headed into the barn, saying, "There are too many things you guys here won't talk about. I wonder if either of you really care that much about stopping the yeti."

Peder grabbed his arm; normally such a move might have caused Rook to react with at least a hint of violence, but he had come to like the old Norwegian and knew the gesture contained no threat. The old man said, "If you believe nothing else, Stanislav, believe that I want it stopped."

The intensity in the man's eyes shone through even in the dull light. Rook threw up his hands. "I give up. I should have stayed in Russia."

"Yes, Stanislav, I have told you that more than once. So what are you and Fossen up to?"

"Your sources didn't tell you?"

"Word about you and Eirek talking for ten minutes in the street passes easily. The substance of your conversation behind closed doors does not."

"We're gonna use the wolves to get to the creature. Fossen's got some kind of tracking device on them, and he's convinced they encounter the creature just about every night."

"What did he think of your plan to capture a wolf?"

"At this point, I'd be perfectly happy to just shoot the creature and be done with it. Capturing a wolf is just a backup plan."

The sound of an engine made its way to Rook's ears. He looked at Peder and saw that the old man had heard it too. Peder said, "That is Thorsen's car. Driving fast, too, by the sound of it. I wonder what is going on?"

They walked out in time to see headlights flash into the short driveway. A man got out, long white hair flowing like something out of a Biblical scene from an old movie. His face was flushed in the high beams.

Peder reached for his extended hand. "Thorsen, what has happened?"

"It's Greta, she—" His eyes squeezed shut and he couldn't continue.

Rook could feel a tentacle of ice start to make its way from the base of his spine upwards. He knew what was coming next. Peder put his other hand on Thorsen's shoulder. "What is wrong with Greta?"

The old man's eyes opened, tired orbs with reddened vessels. "She's dead."

"My friend, how did this happen?"

Thorsen looked up, but this time his eyes met Rook's, not Peder's. "It happened last night. It was the creature."

Another townsperson dead. Rook had watched Peder lead Thorsen Ellefsen into the house, and he could tell the two men shared a bond of long friendship. He had given them some time before following them in. Peder explained that Thorsen's wife, Greta, had been discovered in the bushes behind her house with her throat torn out, just like the two earlier villagers.

Now, Rook sat in the dark in the barn, waiting for Fossen's arrival. He smeared grease on his face and planned his strategy for the rest of the night.

Whatever protection the wolves had offered the town was now out the window. That had never made sense to him anyway, but he'd figured the presence of the wolves meant something. Maybe he'd find out, but for now he would follow the basic plan that Fossen had laid out, with a few minor twists of his own.

At exactly ten o'clock, the headlights of Fossen's S Class Mercedes sent narrow rays of light around the edges of the barn door. Rook jumped to his feet and went outside. Peder had done the same, and the three of them sat at the table in Peder's kitchen. Rook picked up the AR-15 that Fossen had brought.

"Yeah, this should do just fine. If this doesn't take him out, I don't know what will."

Fossen smiled. "Agreed. And Stanislav, here is the walkie-talkie. As soon as I get back to the house and check the tracking device, I will let you know where to start." He reached into his pocket and pulled out an object about the size of a U.S. quarter.

"This is one of the tracking implants. You will need to carry it so I can tell where you are relative to the wolves."

Rook was accustomed to taking long distance orders and being monitored, but that was with Deep Blue, someone he trusted implicitly. Blindly following Fossen's commands went against his instincts.

"Are you sure you don't just have a portable monitor I can carry? It'll make things a lot easier."

"My equipment is large because it is old and designed for multiple purposes. But I assure you it will work just fine. I even have an ear-piece you can plug into the walkie-talkie to keep your hands free."

Rook took the tracking implant from Fossen. "Okay, it'll have to do. When you give me instructions, make sure you don't just tell me where to go. Tell me how close I am to the wolves, what kind of behavior you're seeing, any natural features you know about where I am. The more I can picture the scene, the better off we'll be."

"Agreed." Fossen turned to Peder. "I assume you heard about Greta."

Peder nodded, eyes weary. "Thorsen came up here and

told me himself. Do you still think the wolves can protect us?"

For just a second, Rook noticed tension in Fossen's forehead and neck, but when he answered, his voice sounded calm. "No, Peder, I think something has changed. Perhaps the presence of our friend Stanislav here has disrupted things."

Rook clenched one fist at his side and didn't bother masking his irritation. "So it's my fault?"

Fossen said, "Of course not. I merely meant that you are what has changed. We are fortunate to have you here to help us."

"You don't have anyone else in town that could do this?"

"I could do it myself. But let's be honest. You are a soldier, this is the kind of thing you are training for. Among us, we have plenty of military experience but no one in this town has been on active duty in the past decade. And while hunting has played a key role in our culture for centuries, big game is not something we get the opportunity to confront very often."

Rook couldn't argue with his logic. "Works for me. Are you ready to head back and kick this off?"

Fossen handed Rook one more item, a headpiece with a powerful lamp in the middle. "This should also help keep your hands free.

"Thanks."

Fossen stood up. "Of course. And now I'll return. Peder, between Stanislav and myself, we will deal with whatever this is. You have my word."

Peder's weariness didn't lift when he looked at Fossen. "Eirek, I hope you are right."

When Fossen left, Rook asked Peder, "How's Thorsen taking it?"

Peder snorted. "How would you take the loss of your wife of fifty-two years? He is angry and sad at the same time. He is wondering…" Peder stopped.

"Wondering what?"

Peder shrugged. "It's not important. You need to get ready."

Rook stood, holding the AR-15 as he did. "Yes I do. I have to test out this weapon. Do you have any trees you don't mind getting reduced to sawdust?"

"Pick any tree you want."

"Peder, don't worry. I've come up against far worse than this. Fossen might be out of his depth, but I'll take care of your problem."

Peder's nod seemed an afterthought. "Stanislav, Fossen is not nearly as incapable as he makes it seem. There is some threat from this creature beyond the obvious, that's the only explanation for his actions."

"I was thinking the same thing. What could that be, though? An eight foot hominid tearing people and animals apart is bad enough."

"When you discover the answer, Stanislav, you might finally be able to kill it. If it does not kill you first."

8

Things started to go to hell at two in the morning. In horror movies, midnight is the most dangerous time, but in Rook's experience, you could always count on the worst stuff to go down a couple hours later. Right when most people's energy is at its low point.

It took until midnight for Rook and Fossen to settle into a rhythm. Via the walkie-talkie, Fossen directed Rook through a flurry of turns, and Rook had to focus to keep a picture in his mind of his current location relative to the town and Peder's farm. The wolves did not move fast, stopping every few minutes, and Fossen kept Rook a quarter mile away from them and downwind.

Right at two, as Rook stood waiting for Fossen to tell him the wolves had begun moving again, he sensed something changing. As much of a man of direct action as Rook had always been, he knew from experience to trust his instincts in battle. He bent his knees slightly, getting himself that much more ready for whatever might be coming.

Fossen's voice came through the ear piece, excitement clear even through the static. "Stanislav, they are running now, at twenty-five miles an hour."

"It's about time. What direction?"

"They are running directly toward you."

Rook considered his next move. *Was the creature chasing the wolves? How far behind them was it?*

He readied the AR-15, and listened. Soon, he could hear a faint rustling sound beyond the background noise of the wind. The sound grew clearer, and while it was not loud, he recognized it as the sound of the wolves running. A moment later, the strong beam of the headlamp picked up first the large black wolf and then the others.

They continued to run straight at him. Rook looked behind them, trying to see if the creature followed. He saw nothing there, but his peripheral vision picked up the wolves stopping about fifty feet away. He returned his attention to the large black wolf, the pack leader.

The wolf sniffed the air, then growled while glaring at Rook. Rook grinned at him. *I see you remember me. Smart wolf. Move along now and let the big boys play.*

The pack leader let out a howl, not as loud as the one on that first night, but loud enough to drown out all other sound. Then he charged toward Rook, with the other wolves following.

Not so smart after all. This time I won't be messing around with the knife.

Rook raised the weapon, his finger ready to unleash a fully automatic storm, when suddenly the lead wolf stopped again. Rook held his fire, then became aware of two things.

One: The wolves were cowering, a couple of them even whimpering.

Two: A horrible rotting smell filled his nostrils.

Oh shit, this is not good. Rook put the pieces together in his mind. The wolves had begun to run away, and Rook whirled, leading with the AR-15.

The barrel of the gun smashed into something, and one of

Rook's feet slipped as he tried to catch his balance. He inhaled the fetid stench, heard a massive roar, and felt the AR-15 pulled from his grip. Then giant fingers wrapped themselves around his rib cage and he flew through the air, landing in the frozen thorns of the undergrowth.

He got to his feet and saw the monster running, the weapon looking like a toy in its right hand. The wolves had reached the end of the range of his headlamp, but the giant creature looked to be making up ground. Rook almost felt sorry for the wolves.

He thought, *How the hell did it sneak up on me? Ah, that's right, I was downwind of the wolves, so upwind of him, it makes sense.*

He tapped the headset button. "Hey Fossen, I lost 'em."

"I can see that, Stanislav. What happened?"

"I got caught, couldn't smell the creature until it was too late. And he took my gun."

Silence greeted the observation, before Fossen said, "That is unfortunate. Perhaps we had better rethink this."

Rook began to run while he talked. "Fuck that, I'm going after 'em. Tell me where they're headed, just like before."

"What about the gun?"

"I'll just have to get it back, won't I?"

"Stanislav, how do you expect to manage that?"

"Don't know. Don't care. First I have to catch 'em. Am I going the right direction?"

"Yes."

"Good. Tell me when I need to turn or slow down, Okay?"

"I cannot let you do this."

"I'm doing it with or without you. If I don't need the tracking chip any more, I'll put it down and we can come back and get it later. Otherwise, tell me where to go next. I can still smell it, so that tells me I'm going the right way."

"Fine, Stanislav, do not blame me if you get yourself killed."

"If I get killed, I promise you won't hear a word from me."

"The wolves are slowing. I am not sure what it means."

"How far away are they?"

"About half a mile."

"I'm on it."

Rook picked up his pace. Running wasn't his favorite activity, but with his training he could go quite a way if he paid careful attention to his effort. Right now, he needed to close the gap.

A few minutes later, Fossen announced that Rook was back to four hundred yards away. The wolves were once again ambling around at low speed. Rook could still smell the creature, and he wondered where it had gone.

He turned off his light. He had no idea what kind of senses the creature had, but he figured no reason to make it any easier. The moon provided enough light for him to make his way over the rough ground safely. Three minutes later, he stopped, surprised. The wolves were right in front of him.

He tapped the headset and whispered. "Hey Fossen, why didn't you warn me to stop? They're right here!"

He received no response. After a minute, he swore to himself. *Goddamned Fossen, what's he up to now?*

Rook figured that after initially winding his way uphill away from both the town and the ocean, he was now descending toward town again. This time, he was coming from the other side of the small ridge at the end of the narrow peninsula where the town lay, and he had not yet seen this area.

The wolves still didn't move. They sat in a circle, snouts pointed to the sky, making no sounds that Rook could hear. The stench of the creature remained, but Rook couldn't tell if it indicated a current presence or a prior one. His nostrils had developed a certain amount of tolerance for the horrific odor, which made it more difficult to determine the proximity of the source. He felt exposed, cut off from Fossen's input, unsure if a huge and now armed hominid waited in the surrounding darkness. He had to do something to get back the initiative.

He considered what had happened earlier. The giant hands had tossed him aside, but hadn't done much damage. If the monster had wanted him dead, he'd be dead. Also, it had taken the gun, a deliberate action that showed some of the intelligence Rook had suspected in his first encounter with it the previous evening.

So what the hell is it up to? Maybe...something with the wolves?

Rook nodded to himself, an idea forming. He knew what he needed to do. If he was right, his action would bring about swift—and possibly fatal—consequences, but that was better than standing here waiting. He switched his light back on. Then in one motion, he pulled out his Desert Eagle and took aim at the large black wolf fifty yards away.

As he expected, a roar erupted from the bushes, and even as he fired, he jumped to the right, away from it. His bullet flew a few inches above the wolf's head, exactly as intended. He stowed the pistol in its holster, knowing it would do nothing for him now. Then he turned so the headlamp picked up the creature.

It flew past the spot where Rook had stood a moment earlier, but it kept its gaze right on Rook. There was no mistaking the intent conveyed by its round yellow eyes. Rook knew he had to stay out of its grasp long enough to get the angle he needed, at least if he considered it a priority to keep his arms and legs attached to his torso.

He ran for a tree he'd seen in the headlamp earlier. The trees around here were sparse, and those that managed to grow mostly stood no higher than ten feet. This one was taller, and appeared to have a few branches large enough to support Rook's weight.

He could hear the roar and feel the ground shaking from the footsteps behind him. As he jumped onto a branch about four feet off the ground, he felt something strike his shoulder, knocking him off balance. He managed to get both hands onto a branch above his head, and allowed his body to swing forward until his legs were flying over his head. For a split second, he felt like a gymnast delivering the winning routine—until he crashed down onto the branch and had to hold on tight to keep from falling. *Guess I didn't stick the landing*, he thought.

Ten feet below, the creature still roared, and Rook quickly moved up to a branch three feet higher. Now he was out of range of even those long arms. He steadied his breathing and pulled out the Desert Eagle. The gun had proven ineffective the previous evening, but everything had vulnerable spots.

He felt the tree shake and grabbed the trunk with his free hand to steady himself. The monster had wrapped his massive arms around the base of the tree and was straining with the effort. Rook didn't wait any longer to yell toward the ground.

"Hey, ape man. Look at me when I'm talking to you!"

The creature looked up, fury evident in the glare of the headlamp. Rook fired three shots from the Desert Eagle at its eye socket.

All three shots hit, and Rook felt the yeti's roar reverberate. It let go of the tree and grabbed its head with both hands. Rook couldn't tell whether he'd penetrated the brain, but he'd know soon enough.

The creature stumbled away and dropped to its knees. Rook leapt from the tree, Desert Eagle still in his right hand. He didn't waste ammunition firing at the hobbled figure, but he kept his weight on the balls of his feet, shifting from one foot to the other. The creature jumped to its feet a moment later.

Rook thought, *Well, I guess I didn't hit the brain.*

The creature charged. Rook unloaded with the Desert

Eagle at its legs, but it didn't slow down. He prepared both for impact and to leap sideways to minimize it.

Then an explosive shot rang out. The yeti's hand went down to its left leg and it whirled to the right. Rook's headlamp followed and he saw a sight that did not entirely surprise him: Eirek Fossen holding an AR-15.

The creature ran at Fossen. Even with the pronounced limp from Fossen's shot, it covered ground faster than Rook could have. To his credit, Fossen seemed prepared for it, and dove out of the way. A wide swipe of the creature's paw missed the Norwegian by inches, but the AR-15 flew out of Fossen's hands. Rook launched himself at the weapon, hoping he wasn't too late.

Rook rolled and grabbed it in one motion, ending up on his feet. He fired a dozen rounds at the creature, which had changed directions and was nearly upon Fossen. The yeti roared, but the impact of the shots knocked it to the ground, away from Fossen.

The creature kept rolling after falling, and suddenly it disappeared from the beam of Rook's headlamp. He ran toward the last spot where he had seen it and had to stop before he went over a steep embankment. Looking down, the creature continued to roll, now thirty feet away. Rook fired a few more shots, but he doubted he had hit it.

He started down the slope. Remaining upright proved difficult, as it was nearly a cliff. He established a rhythm, but he knew he couldn't keep up with something hurtling out of control toward the bottom.

When the ground flattened out, he stopped and scanned the area, but saw no sign of the creature. No bloodstains, no trampled vegetation, nothing. He cursed to himself. *Fucking impossible. The bastard is here somewhere.* Several minutes of exploration turned up no additional evidence. The thing had vanished.

Rook's mood became fouler as he worked his way back up the embankment. Twice now, he'd failed to kill it. This time they'd had it in their sights, and a dozen bullets hadn't been enough. As he came over the top, Fossen was peering over the edge. Rook put his palm into the Norwegian's chest, pushing him back.

"Why the hell didn't you stay with the radio?"

Fossen seemed surprised, and stumbled backwards. "Once you lost your weapon, I figured you needed backup more than you needed me telling you where to go."

Rook grunted. "You arrived at the right time, I'll give you that."

Fossen nodded. "As did you. I suspect you saved my life. Just as I arrived, I saw you fire at the wolf. Why?"

Rook tasted sweat as he smiled. "The behavior wasn't making any damn sense unless the creature was doing the opposite of what we thought. I played a hunch and I was right."

"Right about what?"

"Remember how you thought the wolves were chasing it? How its presence incited them to attack? What I saw suggested something different.

"The yeti was protecting the wolves from me."

9

Once again, Rook went to sleep far closer to morning than evening. He hadn't said much to Fossen during the drive back up to Peder's barn, and he'd sensed that both of them were analyzing the events of the prior hour. The other man's attempt to shoot the creature had saved Rook some pain, at a minimum, and besides appreciation, Rook now felt certain of Fossen's commitment to destroying it. Whatever other agendas the man had, Rook felt more confident in teaming up with Fossen for this purpose.

After waking up just before noon, Rook considered what he knew, while sitting at Peder's table drinking tea. Peder said, "Tell me again why you think the creature is protecting the wolves."

"It could easily have killed me, but instead it tossed me aside and ran toward them. Then when I aimed the rifle, it came at me right away. It's the only explanation."

"Maybe it just doesn't like guns."

Rook looked up at Peder and saw the traces of a smile. He chuckled. "Maybe. Anyway, I know we injured it, but I can't figure out where it disappeared to so quickly."

Peder didn't answer for a time, instead staring off to Rook's left. Then he sighed, all signs of the smile evaporated. "Did you ask Eirek?"

"Yeah. Eirek said he had no idea. That slope continues on down to the ocean, right, on the other side of the point?"

"As far as I know, it does. I do not spend any time over there."

"Well, I'll be spending some time there this afternoon. Only thing I can think of to try is checking out the area in daylight, see if I missed anything last night. Even if I can just track the thing a bit further than the bottom of the embankment, it could be a clue to where it went. I'm starting to think the only way we kill this thing is to surprise it in its lair."

"You might be right."

Rook stood up. "So can I borrow your car again? You need it for anything?"

"No, Stanislav, I do not need it. Take it, and be careful."

The old man looked weary to the bone, so different from that first night when he'd performed the nasal swab on Rook with the shotgun. Not for the first time, Rook suspected that the events of the past days had exposed tension the town's residents had managed to keep under wraps for a long time.

Gotta love small towns. They seem so simple on the surface, but poke around a little and skeletons tumble out everywhere. I wonder what the hell is going on.

Rook patted Peder's shoulder with his hand, feeling real affection for the Norwegian. Whatever secrets remained unrevealed, his instincts told him that Peder was the kind of man he could expect to do the right thing when the going got tough. "Looks like my showing up has made your life more difficult, huh?"

Peder's eyebrows rose, and the sad smile showed more resignation than anything else. "Well, at least one good thing has come of it."

"What's that?"

"The creature has been so busy with you that my animals have been safe three nights in a row."

Rook stopped the car in town. The road ended there, so he would make his way on foot back to the spot where the yeti had disappeared. First, he wanted to touch base with Fossen about what they would try that night.

When he parked the car, he looked around at the houses. Their proximity to each other gave the area a similar feel to many small village centers he'd encountered around the world, but the lack of indication of any kind of sales or trade stood out.

He'd only walked a few feet from his car when Anni, the woman who ran the "store" where he'd gotten food that first day, appeared in the sidewalk with two small children clinging to her skirt. Her eyes still carried the same worry they had earlier, but she smiled at Rook and held out her hand.

"Hello, Stanislav. I want to thank you for your help in fighting that monster."

After the cold reception initially, this new appreciation surprised Rook, but he knew that sometimes people take a while to warm up. *Especially when an unknown beast is ripping bodies apart.*

He took the offered hand. "I'm happy to help. We'll take care of it, don't you worry." He leaned down toward the children. "Who are these little ones?"

The two children squirmed behind their mother, and Rook couldn't blame them. What child wouldn't be scared of an unknown stranger who towered over their mother and had a face marked by bruises and cuts? Anni said, "Children, please say hi to Stanislav."

Rook stopped leaning down and laughed. "It's OK."

He sensed another figure behind him and had to resist the

instinct to whirl with the Desert Eagle drawn. It was better safe than sorry in the field, but he didn't expect any threat here to come from someone on the street. He did turn, and he saw two men stop a few feet away as soon as he did. They looked to be in their fifties, both with the light hair and features common to northern Europe.

One of them cleared his throat. "Ah, hello. We wanted to thank you."

The other man nodded. Rook took a step toward them and reached out his hand, "You're welcome. I'm Stanislav. And you are?"

The first man took his hand, hesitating as if unaccustomed to the gesture. "I am Baldur, and this is Roald."

"Well, nice to meet you both. I'm actually heading to see Eirek right now."

Rook turned back to find Anni and the children back at the door of the building in which Rook and Peder had met her that first day, but still watching him. Several more doors had opened on both sides of the street, with individuals watching him from doorways. He figured this was progress after yesterday's experience with faces pressed to the glass of windows.

Shortly before he reached Fossen's house, a man came out of a doorway and didn't stop at a distance like the others. Rook recognized him as Thorsen, Peder's old friend who had just lost his wife to the beast. The white hair flowed behind him as he hurried toward Rook, and tears flowed down his cheeks. He grasped Rook's right hand in both of his.

"Stanislav, you must kill whatever took my Greta."

Rook put his left hand over Thorsen's arthritic digits. "Don't worry, I plan to do just that."

Thorsen looked up at him, then embraced him. "God bless you, son. God bless you."

For one of the few times in his life, Rook was unsure what

to do. Especially compared with the reserve exhibited by the others in town, this show of emotion with everyone watching made Rook uncomfortable. *Well, I guess the man did just lose his wife...*

Then he heard a whisper from Thorsen, words that didn't register until several seconds after Thorsen uttered them. "Pay attention to the victims."

A moment later, Thorsen disengaged himself. He met Rook's gaze for a moment, and his eyes told Rook that his message had been deliberate and the emotional display at least partially an act. Then Thorsen shuffled back to his doorway.

Rook breathed in, trying to keep himself focused. The message clearly was something Thorsen felt he couldn't come right out and say. Therefore, Rook wouldn't mention it to Fossen. But he pondered the words as he reached Fossen's doorstep.

He must mean victims of the beast. But they're dead, right?

Fossen opened the door, one of his arms in a sling. "Stanislav, how are you recovering from last night?"

Entering the house, Rook answered. "Nothing to recover from, just a few bruises. Looks like you weren't so lucky."

Fossen barked a laugh. "Apparently I am not as young as I once was. I woke up this morning with severe pain in my shoulder. The creature didn't get me, but I landed wrong when I dove out of the way. Have a seat, Stanislav. So, what's next?"

"I'm gonna go explore the area where the bastard disappeared last night. I don't know what I'll find, maybe nothing, but he's got to have been losing blood, so I can look for some kind of trail."

Fossen didn't say anything right away, and Rook could almost see his mind calculating. Finally, he said, "I do not believe there is anything out there, but of course I agree that it makes sense for you to have a look around now. What about tonight? Do you want to give it another try?"

"Hell yes. Maybe I'll discover something now that can help us, but even if I don't, we'll hunt again tonight. A thought occurred to me, though. Does your tracking data show any situations where the wolves tend to return to the same place at the same time on multiple nights?"

"Hmm, I have noticed that they roam in big circles, but I had not checked that specifically. I can look into it and let you know tonight."

Rook stood up. "Sounds good. Ten o'clock at the barn again?"

Fossen nodded, "Ten o'clock it is. And Stanislav?"

"What?"

"Be careful."

"Fossen, it's the middle of the day and I won't be that far from town. What is there to be careful of?" Rook's sarcasm was impossible to miss. He didn't need a babysitter.

"I am just saying that there are many unanswered questions, and I suspect last night's activities have increased the risks. An injured animal is a more dangerous animal."

Rook took the Desert Eagle out of the holster, removed the magazine, and jammed it back in. Then he looked at Fossen.

"In case you haven't noticed, I'm not exactly a defenseless cow."

The bottom of the embankment looked far different in the daylight. The area was pancake-flat, a contrast to the constantly sloping terrain everywhere else within a few miles of town. It struck Rook as odd, but he started a methodical search, moving back and forth along the base of the hill.

During his first pass, he didn't find much. He found it hard to believe that the creature wouldn't leave behind some traces of blood, given the number of shots Fossen had landed in its lower body. A faint trace of the stench remained in the air, but it didn't seem stronger in any one part of the area, so its presence didn't help much.

Rook ended his search grid at the top of another steep down-slope. This one dropped to the ocean, water lapping at the rocks at the bottom. He climbed down to only a few feet above the waves and looked up along the rocks in all directions, but he didn't see anything. By the time he climbed back up, he was sweating hard.

He began another search grid, exactly in reverse of the one he had done initially. Back and forth he went, growing more frustrated as each sweep ended. Tasks requiring this level of patience were not his strong suit. Then, he stumbled on a clue.

His boot hit a rock and he tensed his legs to steady himself. Looking down, he saw something glinting in the fading sunlight. He bent over to pick it up, but realized that it wouldn't move. So he got to his knees and started trying to uncover the dirt and soil from around it.

Eventually, he extracted an eighteen-inch long piece of stainless steel, about ten inches wide. It had a lip around the edge, as if it was intended as a cover for something. But he had no idea for what.

When he lifted it up, he got a glimpse of something falling to the ground, and he patted the ground with his hands, trying to find it. His hands settled on an oval object about three inches on the long side.

The object seemed like a necklace charm or medal. He wiped the dirt off it and could make out the image of a sword wrapped in a double-stranded bow. Around the perimeter was some sort of writing, a lot like Norse runes. As he examined it further, he realized that the letters were actually regular western alphabet letters, just styled with runic shapes.

It seemed like the letters formed two words. The first was

fairly easy to make out, the word "Deutsches." German. A bit odd to find here, but the events of World War II had touched all of Europe.

It took him longer to determine the other word, as the letters did not seem to form a word he had seen before. Even assuming it was German, another language he spoke fluently, the meaning didn't jump out at him. After a while, he felt certain he had figured the word out, but he didn't recognize it. And he had no idea how or if this related to the creature. Probably just some decades-old trash.

Still, the medal had an ominous feel to it. The sword combined with the word "German" suggested something military, but the runic lettering lacked any sense of it being official. He could ask Fossen, but he thought perhaps he'd ask Peder first. Fossen was proving himself, but Rook couldn't forget Fossen's attitude that first day.

He put the medal in his pocket, stood up and continued with his grid search. He found nothing else of note. Whatever method the creature had used to escape remained unknown. No blood, no trail, no sign of the missing AR-15.

Rook made his way back to town carrying the piece of stainless steel. He would ask Fossen about that and show the medal to Peder when he returned to the barn. In his head, he repeated the strange word from the medal, trying to work out where he'd seen it before. He didn't know, but the more he pondered it, the more it sounded sinister. A word from somewhere in the past.

Ahnenerbe.

10

Most of the way up the road to Peder's house, Rook heard a gun shot. The right front tire of the car blew out at the same time, and Rook wrenched the wheel to keep from hurtling off the cliff into the ocean. When the car came to a stop, he pulled out the Desert Eagle, opened the driver's door, and kept himself low to the ground when he exited.

After several minutes, he hadn't heard any additional shots. But he didn't dare make his way around to the damaged wheel, exposed as he was to anyone on the hill that rose away from the road. He had no choice but to either wait, or make the rest of the journey on a flat tire.

Rook had never liked waiting. So five minutes later, he was back at the house. He knocked on the door, and Peder let him in.

"Car trouble?"

"If you call having a tire shot out car trouble, then yeah."

Peder exhaled. "Trouble seems to follow you, doesn't it? What does the woman in your life think?"

"Trouble's got me pegged, you're right about that, but there's not really a woman in my life like you mean. Not yet."

Peder just looked at him. "Perhaps that is the problem."

Rook almost opened his mouth to protest, but Peder's words set him thinking about the two women in his life. Well, three if you counted Sara Fogg, the CDC scientist who had accompanied Chess Team as an honorary "pawn," and the girlfriend of the team's leader, King. But the two main ones were Fiona Lane, and his fellow team member Queen.

Fiona was the fourteen-year-old girl the team had saved, the last living speaker of an ancient language that the team had discovered contained great power. King was serving as her guardian, but the whole Chess Team regarded her as family, and though Rook wouldn't have admitted it, he enjoyed his role as Uncle Stan.

As for Queen, well that particular woman in his life didn't have any problem with the trouble that seemed to follow Rook around. Dealing with it was her job as well, and she managed it better than anyone. Rook suspected that trouble would follow him no matter who was in his life, and he wouldn't have wanted it any other way.

Rook became aware that he had paused the conversation. "I doubt it. Anyway, do you have any idea who would want to shoot out my tires? It can't have been Fossen, I just left him and he wouldn't have had time. Plus, whatever other agenda he has, I think he really wants me alive long enough to kill the creature. And I actually got some smiles from the folks in town today."

"Smiles, huh? You are making progress. My answer is that I do not know who would shoot at you, but I am not surprised. Most people here do not like outsiders, even well-intentioned outsiders. Did anything happen today that might explain it?"

"Well, I did find something out where our hairy friend disappeared, but not a lot. First thing was this piece of metal. Fossen suggested that it looked like a cover for one of the older storage units in his lab for biological waste, and perhaps it was debris from when he'd done some modernization a few years back."

Peder looked at the piece of steel. Rook could tell he recognized it and was struggling with how to respond. Rook didn't give him time. "Before you decide whether to lie or say you can't talk about it, let me show you what else I found. This I didn't show to Fossen."

He produced the medal from his pocket and handed it to Peder. The old man's hands shook when he took it, and Rook didn't think it was due to old age. "I don't know what *Ahnenerbe* means. But I have a feeling that in addition to relating to these secrets you can't talk about, both of these items are clues to where the creature is hiding. What do you say to that?"

Peder met his eyes. "I say that you are right on all counts. And that I can't help you."

"Do you know what *Ahnenerbe* means?"

"Yes I do. It is the name of a former German organization, formed during World War II. They primarily focused on the search for historical evidence and proof of German superiority."

Rook nodded several times in succession. "Ah, I knew I'd heard it somewhere. Were they the ones who did human experimentation?"

"I believe so, though I do not think it was their primary focus."

"So what is this medal doing in Norway?"

"Stanislav, many Norwegians fought in the war. I was too young by just a few years, but nearly every man of the correct age in Fenris Kystby fought against the Germans. Such a medal would have been a prized trophy of war."

"Assuming you're right, how did it wind up under this steel cover so far from town?"

"That I do not know."

Rook regarded Peder. He could sense the man's resolve to

keep the town's secrets weakening. *Time to play my last card, at least my last one for now. If this doesn't get him talking nothing will.*

Rook said, "I ran into your friend Thorsen today."

"How is he?"

"Very sad. He broke down in tears on the street and thanked me for trying to kill the creature. Then he embraced me. It was sort of awkward with half the town watching."

Something about the story didn't sit well with Peder. He tried to hide his confusion, saying, "I can see how that would have been awkward. The man is grieving and not in his right mind."

"The thing is, he told me something in a surprisingly clear voice. He said, 'Pay attention to the victims.' Would you happen to have any idea what he meant? I got the impression he didn't want anyone to know he said anything, hence the touchy feely charade."

Peder put his hands on his head and didn't say anything. Rook could tell he was suffering and he didn't have to try hard to allow compassion to enter his voice. "Peder, I don't want anyone else to die because of your secrets."

A moment later, Peder looked up. "It is too late for that. But I will tell you what he meant about the victims."

Peder straightened his back, as if finally telling some of the story would lighten whatever weighed on him. Rook waited.

"Stanislav, three people have been killed by the beast. First was Trond Hagen, a young man who came to this town only about a decade ago. Second was Steinar Dahlberg. And finally, Greta."

"So three people were killed. What's the point, Peder?"

"The point is that all three people were scientists. And all three currently or formerly worked for Eirek Fossen."

Peder's revelation did not surprise Rook. It made sense that the creature's motive would somehow tie into Fossen, the man who controlled the town. Nevertheless, Rook remained silent as he digested the new information.

He was glad he did, because Peder continued. "There is something else. Those three victims were not the only ones who worked for Eirek. My Ilsa did also."

Rook asked, "Who is Ilsa?"

Peder sighed, and his eyes watered. "Ilsa was the most beautiful woman in the world. For fifty years, I was lucky enough to be married to her. Ilsa was my wife."

Rook phrased the next question in as gentle a tone as he could manage, though he imagined he already knew the answer. "What happened to her?"

Peder's voice cracked. "She died two years ago. Brain cancer. By the time we took her to see a doctor in the city, it was too late."

Rook put a hand on the old man's shoulder. "I'm sorry."

Peder nodded, then kept talking. "If the creature is killing those who worked for Eirek, maybe that is why it is targeting my animals. It won't kill me, since I didn't actually work for him."

Rook thought Peder could be right, but he also though the Norwegian was being too hard on himself. "Or maybe the damn thing is just hungry. Don't worry about the reasons, just focus on how we stop it."

Peder stared at him, and might have dipped his chin, Rook couldn't tell. Then he lifted himself off the couch and went through the door into his bedroom without a word. Rook let out a breath before he got up and headed out to the barn. *That old man is seriously hurting.*

He turned his thoughts to killing the creature. Rook and Fossen had agreed not to start their next round of stalking until midnight, when Fossen would contact Rook via walkie-talkie to let him know where the wolves were. Nothing had happened before that time on previous evenings, so they didn't see the need to waste a lot of time wandering.

Rook, however, had no intention of sitting in Peder's barn until that time. Leaving the tracking chip behind, at eight o'clock he made his way down to the area where the creature had disappeared the night before. Specifically, Rook went to the tree he'd climbed, which had enough upper branches to conceal him. He climbed the tree again and settled in the elbow of a branch near the top of it, a spot from which he had a clear view of the top of the embankment.

Night vision goggles would have really helped on this mission. If he could have enlisted Deep Blue and the satellites at his disposal, they could have scanned the area for heat signatures and possibly discovered how the monster had escaped. He had none of those options, instead relying on the AR-15, the Desert Eagle and his five senses.

On this clear night, the moon provided enough light that he would be able to see the creature if it came up the embankment. Rook didn't like to wait, and he'd likely spend three hours staking the place out with nothing to show for it. But he couldn't think of any better alternatives.

His mind wandered as he watched. He wondered again if this was what he wanted, wasting time cut off from the world instead of returning to his teammates. This kind of withdrawal wasn't like him, but he'd never failed so utterly at a mission as he had in Russia. The fact that it wasn't his fault didn't ease the bitterness about the outcome. He still didn't feel ready to go home.

Returning his mind to the matter at hand, he considered the victims, as Thorsen had suggested. If he were a detective or a mystery writer, the fact that all three victims worked for Fossen would provide motive. But how intelligent was the thing? How much would motive even be relevant?

Rook didn't know. He did suspect that Greta's death had caused Fossen to change his tune about having Rook in town. With that killing, Fossen had surely figured out that his scientists were targets, and the town's leader would suspect that he might be the next in line. Rook would bet money that Fossen didn't know the creature's origin or where it had disappeared—otherwise Fossen wouldn't need him.

So, Rook could assume the creature had a grudge against Fossen. Aside from indicating that using Fossen as bait might be a good strategy, that fact didn't get him anywhere. Maybe he'd suggest the bait idea tomorrow if tonight didn't pan out.

The creature's obvious protection of the wolves also served to add to the confusion. Combined with the apparent grudge against Fossen, it made Rook wonder if Fossen's "research" had any negative impact on the wolves. The more he considered this, the more likely he thought it, but it didn't help him to know any more about how to find and kill the creature.

Other questions started popping into his head. *Why had Fossen's son tried to kill him the night before Fossen turned friendly? Who had fired the shot at his tire today? Was anything at all in this town what it seemed on the surface?*

Rook knew the answer to the last one was no. As for the rest, he had no clue. Things were spinning out of control, and none of the town's residents with the possible exception of Fossen seemed to sense it. All in all, Rook couldn't have found a more appropriate place for a Special Forces soldier to wind up on vacation.

Around ten o'clock, Rook saw a shadow at the top of the steep grade. A moment later, he could make out the yeti's outline in the moonlight. His hunch had paid off.

Now what do I do?

Rook's plan was to try again to figure out where the creature was coming from. He'd wait until it disappeared, then go back down the hill and not stop looking until he found something. If it took past midnight, Fossen might wonder what the hell was going on when Rook didn't have the sensor, but he'd talk his way around that one. He did have the walkie-talkie with him.

Tonight, the creature moved with a noticeable limp, something Rook noted with satisfaction. *About time, he showed signs of mortality. Thank you, Eirek Fossen, for doing something brave and stupid and firing those shots at it.*

As the creature reached the edge of the clearing where the wolves had circled the previous night, Rook dropped silently from the tree. The odor was strong, and unlike the previous evening, Rook hadn't become accustomed to it yet. Maybe he'd get lucky.

He turned on his headlamp and headed down the embankment. When he reached the bottom, he sniffed, trying to gauge the smell. It was certainly stronger than it had been during the day. Rather than walk a specific grid, he tried to let his nose guide him.

After a few minutes, he had narrowed down a small area from where the smell seemed to originate. It was not as strong as right at the base of the hill, but moving in any direction other than back the way he'd come caused it to weaken considerably. *Right here is where the creature must have come from.*

Looking at the ground, nothing jumped out at him. He'd been over this ground the previous evening and a couple of times earlier today. Aside from a bush about two feet high and five feet in diameter, the frozen ground had no distinguishing features. He examined the bush, pulling back each branch, one by one.

He saw evidence of broken and crushed branches, but he couldn't assume that was due to anything other than some animal trampling it. As he reached its roots, though, he made a discovery: The ground around the roots in the center was solid.

In fact, when he tapped it with his hand, he heard a small reverberation. Scraping away at the dirt, he saw metal glinting in his headlamp. Rook knew with certainty now that the bush was hiding some sort of cover or door.

He considered how to expose it and open it. Perhaps it could be opened only with some sort of remote, but he doubted that. He had resigned himself to scraping away dirt until he found the edges when he noticed that closer to the outer perimeter of the bush, the ground was a little higher than in the center. He stepped back and grabbed the roots nearest to a spot where that difference was noticeable, and he pulled.

He heard a creaking sound, and the bush lifted a few inches off the ground. He didn't have much leverage, and the root slipped out of his hands, dropping the bush back to its former level. He noted how the dirt seemed to drift right into the correct spots to make the seam all but invisible, and he wondered how they managed that.

He got a better grip and tried again, and this time, he lifted it completely, the bush turning sideways as a trap door about four feet square, opened to vertical. He stared down the opening and the creature's odor rushed up at him, causing him to swallow and his eyes to water. Despite the vile smell, he grinned when he saw the ladder descending into the darkness.

He'd struck pay dirt. He had found the yeti's lair.

11

The smell only got worse as Rook descended the ladder. Before he did, he pulled the trapdoor shut, figuring he should cover his tracks to the extent possible. The ladder dropped about twenty feet before ending in a tunnel six feet high. The tunnel was carved from the rock, and crumbled stone littered the bottom of it, suggesting that the tunnel's top might have some structural problems. His feet crunched over the fallen stones as he made his way down the tunnel, away from the ladder.

He had a sense that the tunnel was generally sloping downward in the direction of town. He made slow progress, ducking his head the whole time, but after five or six minutes, he estimated he'd come a quarter mile. He found himself at a metal door with a frame embedded in the rock. The word "Ragnarök" had been stenciled above the door. Rook knew that Ragnarök was a Norse prophecy about the end of the world that included a massive battle in which many of the Nose gods— Thor, Odin, Loki, etc—die. The word actually translates to "Doom of the Gods." The story included the near destruction of the human race, but the survivors would reclaim the Earth, now a paradise. What that had to do with this place, he had no idea, but he was sure that whoever came up with the name had a flare for the dramatic.

The door had no handle, but Rook knew the creature must have a way to get through. The upper right seemed to have a space between the jamb and the door, and Rook was able to use the tips of his fingers to get it open. It took the right combination of leverage and strength, and he couldn't see how a creature with massive hands could pull it off.

The door slammed shut behind him, and Rook took in his surroundings. He was inside some sort of laboratory, and while the equipment seemed ancient, it wasn't in disorder. The smell had gotten even worse, and Rook had to wrap his black handkerchief around his nose to ward off the nausea.

Moving through the room, he went through one of its two doors. This one was just a small storage closet with some crumbling boxes in it. Returning to the room's other door, he came to a larger room, one which encompassed several small offices as well as containing a couple of doors with the universal biohazard stickers on them. Rook moved to one of those doors.

When he did, he heard a howling sound, a pitiful echo of what the wolves outside were capable of, but loud enough in the enclosed space. He put the strap of the AR-15 around his shoulder, readied the Desert Eagle in his right hand and opened the door.

He saw several built-in cages rising to the ceiling, and one of them was not empty. It contained three wolves.

These wolves were nothing like the others, however. Their coats were missing large patches of fur, and they were small and scrawny, every rib visible. Each was deformed in some way, with one having only one eye in the middle of its forehead, another missing an ear and the front left paw and the third with something like a fifth leg dangling from its belly. The animals whimpered as he approached.

Holy shit, Rook thought. *Are these Fossen's experiments?*

He stared at them for another minute, trying to keep his mind off the pain in the animals' eyes. Then he exhaled and left the room without looking back. He could feel the blood draining from his fingers due to the tightness of his grip on the Desert Eagle, and he had to force himself to unclench his hands.

The other biohazard room contained nothing, so Rook moved through the one other door off the main room. Unlike in the previous areas, this new room he entered had a source of natural light, a small window near the top of one of the walls. Despite the ray of light peeking through the top, he saw nothing but dirt packed against the glass outside the window. Under the window, he could see a set of double doors, and he got the impression that this room had once served as the entrance to the whole lab.

Testing out his theory, he tried to open one of the double doors. He did so slowly, which he appreciated a moment later when dirt started falling through the opening. He shined his headlamp through it and just as with the window, he saw nothing but earth on the other side. The conclusion was clear: Someone had buried the main entrance to the lab.

He forced the door closed and looked at the rest of the space. In the corner, he saw a long couch, torn and filthy, with several old blankets on top of it. Near it, he saw a pile of bones and decaying flesh, and he knew these were the animals stolen from Peder's farm.

He approached the couch. *Wow. Yeti's bedroom and kitchen all rolled into one. I hope it isn't his bathroom too, though the smell's so bad already I guess it wouldn't matter.*

On top of the strewn blankets, he saw a faded brown folder. It seemed out of place in the clutter, placed there deliberately. Rook snatched it up, jumping away as he did. He knew he looked foolish and that the idea of a folder triggering a booby-trap was ridiculous, but he'd seen too much craziness in

Fenris Kystby not to use caution.

His heart rate sped up when he saw the logo on the outside of the folder. The same Nazi logo he'd found on the medal earlier in the day. The symbol of the *Ahnenerbe.*

He opened the folder and began to read. It started with documents dated in the 1960s, written in German, but soon the language switched to Norwegian. The documents were what a U.S. corporation would call executive summaries, research results translated into high level conclusions suitable for non-scientists. They pertained to biological experiments, specifically genetic engineering. Rook couldn't tell from these documents what the goals were, but most of the summaries detailed failures. Horrible mutations, stillborn monsters, constant returning to the drawing board.

All the documents bore the same signature, that of an Edmund Kiss, with *Ahnenerbe* scrawled under the signature. Rook considered this. Genetic experiments and a survivor from a Nazi group somehow tied into a remote location in Norway. It didn't sound real, but here he was seeing it with his own eyes.

As he neared the end of the folder, the dates moved into the early nineteen-eighties, and the signatures grew less legible. Rook's eyes were blurring, but he tried to focus, looking for any details that might tell him what had happened at the lab and to Edmund Kiss.

Then he saw it. A summary describing a success. A huge increase in size accompanied by few side effects except increased hair and odor emission. He assumed this was the origin of the yeti, not some experiment gone wrong, but an experiment gone right. They must have started with apes, not wolves, though the documents only used the word "subjects," so it was not clear.

On this document, the handwriting was not recognizable as anything but a scribble. Perhaps Edmund Kiss suffered from progressive arthritis or some other such ailment. Rook turned to the next document, the last one in the folder.

This document was different from the others. It read like a diary entry rather than an official report: And it was written in German, just like the first few documents.

When he read its contents, he stopped breathing.

None of the others, not even my son, had the fortitude to take the necessary steps. The old ones are still waiting for a Führer who will never return, while the young ones know nothing of sacrifice. I am now a living testament to success beyond our wildest dreams.

The wolves responded well physically, but they went mad and we had to destroy them before they chewed off their own limbs. The others thought we simply needed more experiments to get rid of the behavior, but I knew better. Wolves are mad by nature, and the procedure merely enhanced that along with their physical size. Choosing a different subject was the only answer.

My influence has waned, and they rejected this approach. They tolerate me the way one tolerates a lame dog nearing the end of its life. By rights, I should be dead already, but I am convinced that my purpose is to serve the good of the Aryan people and bring about paradise. I experimented on the only subject remaining to me.

Myself.

The results have been astounding. Three months after the transformation, I have more energy than I did even as a young man, along with the strength of ten men. I can feel the madness assaulting my senses, but I hold it at bay through the force of my will.

Fear has replaced their dismissive tolerance, a reversal that pleases me. But I can sense them working up the courage to take some sort of action. I would not be the first to meet with an accident.

I could fight back, but I have no desire to shed the blood of my fellow Aryans. They are the future. I do not know how much life I have left, but I will leave them with all the signs of a lab accident to convince them that I am dead already. I will retreat to the wilderness.

I will confess to a certain amount of vanity in documenting these events. This testament I will place in the old lab, abandoned like so many other things in favor of changes that are not always improvements. Perhaps in the distant future, someone will read these words and understand the depth of true commitment.

Goodbye.

Rook had the answer he'd sought for what seemed like forever, but in reality had only been three days. Maybe a few years back, he would have felt shock and disbelief, but his capacity for surprise had diminished in recent years. This explained an awful lot of things.

The yeti was the result of an experiment by a deranged Nazi—on himself.

12

The only thing still not clear to Rook was why Kiss held a grudge. Had something else happened after he'd written those words? Rook didn't know, but it really didn't impact the task at hand. Now that he had found Kiss's home base, killing him would just be a matter of picking the right moment.

As he lifted the trapdoor with the bush attached, his watch read eleven forty-five. He had to hustle, but he made it back to town by midnight and headed right for Eirek Fossen's house. Fossen answered the door with the walkie-talkie in his hands.

"Stanislav. I was just wondering where you were."

"I'm here, Fossen. I know how we're gonna kill the creature."

Fossen blinked as if trying to process the words, then he stood back and motioned Rook inside. "By all means tell me about it."

Seated at Fossen's table, Rook began to describe what he'd found. The secret entrance and the lab. Rook asked, "Do you know anything about this?"

Fossen remained motionless in his chair. He didn't even appear to blink. Finally, he answered, which seemed to snap him out of it. "The old lab. It was abandoned so long ago, I'd totally forgotten about the escape route. It was something my father, who worked there, told me about when I was a child, but I never actually went into the tunnel myself."

"And it didn't occur to you when the creature disappeared right in that area last night?"

"No. The lab was actually closer to town, as you discovered by your long walk in the tunnel."

"Right. You say your father worked there? Is he still alive?"

"No, he is not. He was already an old man when I was born, and he died in a lab accident."

"Sounds like the lab was a dangerous place. I saw that everything appears to have been buried. Why was that?"

"Memories, Stanislav. It was a symbol of old things that we no longer wished to think about. Perhaps even felt ashamed of. I was still in school when it happened."

"But you still became a scientist yourself, with your own lab. Continuing your father's work?"

Fossen grunted. "Hardly. I'm sure that spending time there as a child contributed to my current interests, but my research is very different than what they were doing."

Rook didn't comment on how unlikely that sounded. "Uh-huh. Well, I did find something else interesting—lab reports. In a folder with a Nazi symbol on it. Is that part of what you wished to forget?"

"You have stumbled on one of our secrets. You can see why this is something we don't talk about."

"You got that right. It seems like work at the lab was not going well. But the last report was different. Instead of a report, it was like a diary entry. From a man named Edmund Kiss."

Fossen froze at the mention of the name, but he didn't pause before answering. "Edmund Kiss. I have not heard that name in a long time."

"Another one of your secrets?"

"Something like that."

"Well, good old Edmund had some interesting news. Apparently, he experimented on himself and turned himself into a giant creature with superhuman strength and a foul stench. Sound familiar?"

"It does, but—"

Rook cut him off. "But Edmund Kiss is dead? Well it turns out that he faked his own death. Something about letting the younger generation have their time."

Fossen grasped the implications of this immediately. "So the creature we are fighting is Edmund Kiss?"

"It sure as hell seems like it. And he's not too happy with you."

"I guess not. Did you find anything else?"

"You mean besides the answer to all your problems? Sure, I found three abominations, pitiful wolves who were obviously the subject of genetic experimentation."

Fossen's eyes grew wide. He cleared his throat and said, "Those must be the wolves that escaped from my lab a few months ago. I see that Kiss took them."

Rook knew there had to be more to the story than that, but he didn't push it. After they killed the creature, he could decide what to do next. If he even stayed in this lunatic asylum of a town. The day's discoveries had finally made him feel like a soldier again, kicking ass and getting the job done. After he killed Kiss, he knew he'd feel even better. But would he be ready to return to Chess Team? He'd ask that question again tomorrow.

"So you're creating genetic freaks with your research. Isn't that dangerous?"

"Come now, Stanislav, you do not strike me as a man who is afraid of progress. Sometimes solving great problems takes great sacrifice."

Rook bit down on the response that came to mind. *What would you know about sacrifice? Edmund Kiss turned himself into a monster. That's a sacrifice. You're just playing God without any real personal stake.*

Fossen didn't appear to notice the pause. "So, we should get him tonight, yes?"

Rook nodded. "Damn right. No guarantees, but I bet he'll return down that ravine. The tree is the only place to hide, so that's where I'll go. I'll have a clear shot with the AR-15 and I should be able to hobble him. Then I can finish him off up close."

"I am coming with you."

"No way, Fossen. We had this discussion before. Plus, didn't we lose the other AR-15?"

"Actually you lost it, but I have another one, so it does not matter. Before, I needed you. Now I can just as easily go hide in the tree and take care of this myself. So maybe the question is, are *you* coming with *me?*"

Rook groaned, but he knew Fossen spoke the truth. The two of them in that tree together could get tense in a hurry. But he didn't trust that Fossen could pull this off by himself, plus Rook had invested enough energy in this fight that he wanted to see it through. "Fine. Just don't get in my way."

"Do not worry, we make a good team."

"So you say. I won't wait for you if we have to run."

Fossen's eyes appeared as intense and cold as they had that first day when Fossen had told Rook to leave town. "I would not have it any other way."

The wolves returned to the clearing at two in the morning. Edmund Kiss followed. The wolves didn't stop this time, they just kept running, but Kiss slowed to a jog at the clearing. From the tree, Rook could see the huge limbs rumbling to a stop. Knowing the truth behind the creature changed everything, and Rook couldn't help feeling sorry for him.

He looked down at the AR-15 and shook his head. Sorry or not, Kiss needed to be put down. There could be no justification for tearing apart a helpless old woman like Thorsen's wife, Greta, no matter what she had done in prior years.

Kiss glanced at the tree, and for a moment, Rook became aware of the exposed position he was in. Next to him, Fossen shifted, and Rook wanted to slap the man to get him to keep still. They had enough firepower to keep Kiss out of the tree, but it could get pretty hairy if it came to that.

Rook let out a breath when Kiss turned and started to the embankment. The instant he disappeared from view, Rook jumped from the tree and started running. He heard Fossen behind him do the same thing, but he no longer had the luxury of focusing on anything except his target.

At the top of the embankment, he stopped, raised the AR-15 and looked down the slope. His headlamp picked up Kiss reaching for the trap door. Rook let off a dozen shots, and he knew some of them had to have hit, but during the barrage, Kiss had disappeared down the ladder, letting the trap door close again as he did.

Fossen came up behind him. "Stanislav, did you get him?"

Rook shook his head. "He's not dead, I'm sure of that. Looks like we follow him down."

They half slid down the hill and hurried to the bush. Rook yanked it open while Fossen aimed his rifle down the hole. They waited a beat, but heard no sound.

Rook slung the strap for the AR-15 over his shoulder, pulled out the Desert Eagle, and went down the ladder. He reached the bottom and whistled for Fossen to follow him. A few seconds later, Fossen reached the tunnel.

"I had no idea this was here."

"Yeah, well, Edmund Kiss did. Stay behind me."

They started moving through the tunnel. Knowing his way now, Rook moved more quickly than he had earlier. About halfway down, he heard a thud from Kiss opening the door to the lab and letting it slam shut. He picked up the pace. Soon they arrived at the door, and he turned to Fossen. "Know why this place was called Ragnarök?"

Fossen looked at the chipping paint above the door, his face blank and unreadable. "No idea."

Rook sighed. *Getting straight and honest answers from these people is like pulling teeth from a Neanderthal.* He turned back to the task at hand. "Here's the drill. You open it. I'll lead with a burst of fire and you stay right behind me."

"What is behind the door?"

"One of the two main labs. Do you remember it?"

"I am sure I was in it, but it was so long ago. Having seen it today already, you know it far better than me."

"OK, here goes. Whenever you're ready."

Fossen yanked the door open from the same upper corner Rook had used to lever it earlier. Rook opened fire with the AR-15 and jumped into the room. Fossen followed. Rook sprayed to both sides, obliterating cabinets and lab equipment with a cacophony of destruction. He saw no sign of Kiss, so he took more steps toward the door into the main lab.

A roar erupted from above him and he cursed at himself for not thinking of it. He whirled, knowing what he'd see. Kiss had managed to hang on the ceiling and drop directly onto Fossen.

The sound of Fossen's head hitting the hard floor told Rook that the town's leader was in some serious trouble. He unleashed another stream of fire at Edmund Kiss's legs, and Kiss staggered off Fossen. He swung a massive clawed backhand toward Rook, and Rook couldn't quite manage to get out of the way while holding the gun. A white-hot surge of pain started in his left shoulder and made a beeline for his brain, causing him to squeeze his eyes shut to ward off the nausea. When he opened them, he saw Kiss disappear through the door, pulling himself with his two hairy arms and dragging ruined legs behind him.

Through watering eyes, he saw Fossen lying still on the ground. He didn't have time to worry about that now; he had to finish Kiss once and for all. For a moment he thought his shoulder was dislocated, but he moved it and didn't pass out from the pain. It hurt like hell, and he would have a hell of a bruise, but he could still hold the Desert Eagle in that hand as a backup. He didn't think it mattered; if the automatic rifle wouldn't do the trick, odds were against the pistol doing it.

He went through the door and didn't see Kiss. Maybe he was hiding in one of the offices or biohazard rooms, but Rook didn't think so. He expected to find the man/monster in the only spot that probably still felt safe, the room where he ate and slept. A trail of blood confirmed this theory. The door to that room was open, and Rook approached it with caution.

From the doorway, he saw Kiss collapsed on the couch and blankets. He could hear wet breathing, and he knew a lucky shot must have gotten through the breastplate and pierced a lung. Kiss turned his head to meet Rook's eyes, but he made no move to stand up.

The eyes no longer seemed monstrous. They were sad, and even though yellow, they felt all too human. Rook raised the AR-15, then lowered it, wincing as the movement on his right side shifted the injured left shoulder. He said, "Edmund Kiss, right?"

Kiss nodded.

"Can you still talk?"

Kiss shook his head and made a breathy sound that could have been "no" if Rook used his imagination a bit.

"I'll do the talking then. You've caused a lot of trouble. Why'd you come back?"

Kiss shook his head again, and Rook wondered what he meant. *You don't want to tell me? You don't know? What?*

Rook felt awkward. He knew that anti-terrorist units faced regular difficulty in identifying the enemy, but usually Chess Team didn't have that problem. Living statues brought to life by the "Mother Tongue" didn't leave any doubt about the need for termination. Here, though…

Rook lowered the gun. Kiss's eyes opened wider. He got himself to a seated position and pointed to his head then to Rook. Rook couldn't believe it.

Damn. He actually wants me to shoot him. What the hell do I do now?

Kiss must have sensed Rook's doubt, because he let out a roar and flung himself off the couch at Rook. His legs wouldn't hold his weight, but the massive body gained enough momentum to take it toward Rook's position. Without even pausing to think about it, Rook pulled the trigger and sent two dozen shells into Kiss's face at point blank range.

Kiss collapsed to the ground, landing on his side, then rolling onto his back. As he did, a hand shot up in the air, and Rook could see that Kiss clutched something in it. Then the hand dropped to the ground. Still several feet away, Rook kept the weapon aimed at Kiss's face.

A minute later, he'd seen no movement, so he shuffled closer. He couldn't hear any breathing, but he wanted to make sure. He poked at the rib cage near the armpit, and the lack of reaction told him he could move closer. Still wary, he put a hand on the old German's chest and felt no heartbeat. Edmund Kiss was dead.

Rook stood, then he remembered the dying move with the

hand. He found what Kiss had been holding, a manila envelope that had seen better days.

He heard movement behind him and turned with the gun. Fossen was in the doorway, on his hands and knees. In one motion, he stowed the rifle and stuffed the envelope under his shirt, then moved toward Fossen.

"You all right, Fossen?"

Fossen shifted so his back leaned against the doorjamb. "I am very dizzy and my head feels like a thousand trains are rolling through it at once. But I believe I escaped serious injury."

"You're one lucky bastard, you know that?"

"Once again you have saved my life. I thank you. And I see you have finally killed our monster."

Fossen stared at the body of Edmund Kiss, and Rook detected some strong emotions. Under the circumstances, he understood that, what with the memory of the dead and the impact of a quarter ton animal landing on him. Fossen inhaled through his nose and then nodded.

"If you don't mind, Stanislav, could you help me to my feet?"

"Sure." Rook helped the man stand up. "You have a doctor in this town?"

Fossen leaned on Rook, unable to stand on his own. "Yes we do. I think I should pay him a visit."

"My left shoulder could use some attention too. Let me help you back through the tunnel."

Before he left the doorway, Fossen took one more look back. He nodded once, and Rook could see again the ice that seemed to come and go from the man's expression. After a moment, Fossen turned, and they began to stagger away, Rook trying to bear Fossen's weight without allowing too much pressure to build on his left side.

Unlike Fossen, he didn't look back.

By the time they arrived in town, Rook's shoulder felt like a crazed drummer was using him for percussion practice. Fossen's balance had improved, and he made it most of the way back without leaning on Rook. As they started by the first houses, people started coming out of the doors. Rook didn't see how they could know that the deed was done, but he figured maybe two battered figures limping down the main drag spoke for itself. Still, at four in the morning, he wouldn't have expected it.

Lights flicked on all the way down the street, and they received nods and varying degrees of smiles from each house. A few people walked out to shake their hands. Anni actually walked out and embraced Fossen, then offered her hand to Rook. He returned her smile along with the handshake.

Soon enough, they reached Peder's car, and Rook stopped.

"Fossen, I think this is where I get off. I need to sleep for a couple days, but I'll settle for a few hours in Peder's barn."

Fossen pursed his lips. "I could offer you a bed in my house, but I sense that you are comfortable where you are, yes?"

"Yeah, I think so. I'm a sucker for the smell of horse shit."

"I believe you are. I will arrange for the doctor to drive up to Peder's house sometime in the late morning."

"Thanks, Fossen."

"Thank-you, Stanislav. You can call me Eirek."

Rook looked into those eyes again, trying to read them. Maybe he was just tired, but Fossen's look didn't give anything away. Fossen had done well tonight, and only Rook's own failure to look up when they entered the first door had allowed the creature to take him out. He didn't trust the man yet, but he'd gained some respect for him.

"Okay, Eirek. And now, I say good night."

Rook sat down in the car and closed the door. He let out a groan as his shoulder moved, the first expression of pain he had allowed himself tonight. Then he put the car in gear.

A couple of minutes out of town, he remembered the envelope. He was weary, and his eyes had started drifting shut, but he didn't want to wait to get to Peder's house to examine its contents. He stopped the car in the middle of one of the lesser inclines, put on the emergency brake, and opened the envelope.

The envelope contained a black and white photograph of about eight by ten inches. The picture contained two figures, and a caption scrawled underneath read "Father's Day." Rook couldn't be certain, but the writing looked an awful lot like those signatures he'd seen so many of when looking through the folder of lab reports earlier in the day.

The father in the photo was a man with hair starting to go gray, with the name Edmund printed under it in a different hand.

The son was around twelve years old; his picture had the name Eirek printed under it.

EPILOGUE

Rook crouched on a cliff halfway between Peder's house and the town. Below him lay the road, and below that another cliff and the ocean. Fenris Kystby lay a mile to his right, just visible through the lifting fog. The rays of the early morning sun sparked as they met the waves, lending the scene a tranquility that Rook welcomed.

But he knew it was an illusion. The past few days had shown him how much conflict lay beneath the town's calm exterior. The question once again was whether he should return to his team or stay just a little bit longer. He was beaten and bruised and not in any condition to hoof his way out of town, but Peder had offered him a ride. The man did his best to make the offer sound innocent, but the underlying tone of "get out while you can" lingered.

Peder wanted him to leave because the old man feared for Rook's life. Even after the serious smack-down he'd delivered to the mad scientist turned yeti. And that meant that whatever secret the town of Fenris Kystby still concealed was even more dangerous. Worse, the man in charge oozed megalomania.

Fossen. He was up to something. But what? And what was

the endgame? All Rook really knew was that the man wasn't alone.

Not one, but two people had tried to kill Rook. He would have bet money that Fossen's son attacked him on Fossen's orders. He couldn't remember the exact sequence of events, but he suspected that Fossen gave the order after first meeting Rook, and didn't manage to rescind it before realizing that he needed Rook's help. *The town had brains*, Rook realized, *but lacked brawn*. With his employees being targeted, Rook thought Fossen must have assumed that the creature got his son, too. Fossen might be questioning that assumption now, given the newly discovered identity of the creature, but all evidence to the contrary had been burned to dust and swept out to sea.

Then there was the second attempt on his life, the shots fired at him as he drove Peder's car. Who had done that? Maybe Fossen had arranged it because he didn't want Rook rooting around where the creature had disappeared. Or maybe Fossen didn't intend to kill him, but had just arranged the shots to keep him focused on his own survival and not thinking too much about the town's secrets. Or hell, maybe Fossen wasn't behind it, maybe someone in the town took a shot because Rook was working *with* Fossen.

The truth was, he had no idea about those shots. One more reason to stick around and find out which heads needed busting for that particular attempt on his life. But even without the attempts on his life, he knew he couldn't leave without getting some more answers about Edmund Kiss and Eirek Fossen. The piece of paper he held in his hand only made him more determined to do just that.

In court, they would have called it a "dying declaration." He had discovered the single sheet of paper behind the photograph in the envelope that Kiss had clutched as he died. It was written in German, in the same scribbled hand as the document he had found during his first visit to the old lab—now rough and nearly illegible, as though written quickly.

Ich hab ihn gesehen, Deinen Wolf. Du musst aufhören. Es ist zu gefährlich Zu schrecklich. Ich kam zurück um Dich aufzuhalten aber ich bin zu spät. Du musst die ---- versiegeln—

Rook had memorized the translation.

I've seen it, your Dire Wolf. You must stop. It's too dangerous. Too horrible. I came back to stop you, but I'm too late. You must seal the ---- or —

Dire wolf? Is he talking about the large black wolf? Rook shook his head. *Couldn't be. He protected them. And seal what?* The old man's chicken scratch was hard to read in general, but that single word was illegible. If only the man had finished the note, which was clearly intended for Fossen and likely regarded his research. The only thing the note made clear was that even the Nazi turned yeti feared Fossen's research, and Rook was pretty sure that Nazi yetis didn't typically fear a whole lot.

Rook stood and wrapped his arms around his chest as a cool breeze flowed down the hillside and plummeted over the cliff. The wind howled for a moment and Rook felt a chill run up his spine. The sensation was momentarily so intense that he nearly dropped to a knee. *That wasn't the wind,* he thought, fighting the shiver. The howl sounded distant. Miles away. Yet it emanated power and fear. He quickly ran through the possibilities.

Not the yeti.

Not the wolves.

I've seen it, your Dire Wolf.

Fossen's research.

The crunch of approaching footsteps snapped Rook's attention away from the distant sound. The wind carried wood smoke and moth balls.

"Peder," he said in greeting.

"Have you decided, Stanislav?"

"Yeah," Rook said. A part of him hated this decision. He'd been gone too long. His team would be worried. Queen would be... Thinking of her was nearly enough to change his mind. But if any member of Chess Team stood in his shoes, they'd see it through, too. Something dangerous brewed in Fenris Kystby and it would eventually find its way to the outside world. *It has to be stopped*, Rook thought. *It's what we do.*

Rook turned to Peder and the old man frowned. He could see Rook's decision in his stone faced expression. Peder sighed, turned and walked away.

"Where are you going?" Rook asked.

Without looking back, Peder said, "To reload my shotgun."

ABOUT THE AUTHORS

JEREMY ROBINSON is the author of eleven novels including PULSE, INSTINCT, and THRESHOLD the first three books in his exciting Jack Sigler series. His novels have been translated into ten languages. He lives in New Hampshire with his wife and three children.

Visit him on the web, here:
www.jeremyrobinsononline.com

EDWARD G. TALBOT is the pen name for two authors. Ed Parrot lives in Massachusetts and has long been fascinated with turning ideas into written words. Jason Derrig lives in Maine and likes to tell stories, especially about conspiracies. The two authors have collaborated to create a brand of thriller that keeps the stakes high while not taking itself too seriously. In addition to the Chess team thriller, their current work includes the conspiracy thriller novel *New World Orders* and the thriller half-novel *Alive From New York*. Their second novel, *2012: The Fifth World*, is available now.

Visit him on the web, here:
www.edwardgtalbot.com

COMING IN 2011

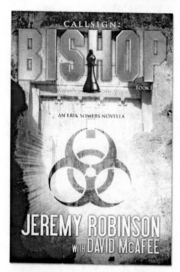

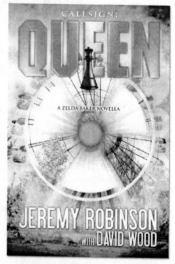

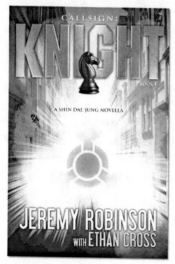

CPSIA information can be obtained at www.ICGtesting.com
Printed in the USA
LVOW041441140912

298871LV00009B/7/P